INSIGHT

by

Marén Klement

 New Generation Publishing

Real People, Real Stories

This book has been produced with assistance from
The London Borough of Barking and Dagenham Library Service
Pen to Print: Real People, Real Stories Creative Writing Project 2016
with funding from The Arts Council, England Grants for the Arts.

Supported using public funding by
**ARTS COUNCIL
ENGLAND**

LOTTERY FUNDED

London Borough of
Barking & Dagenham
lbbd.gov.uk

For Richard

1

The distant mumbling of the engine made him feel sick to his whole body; anxiety winding its way through his veins, entering every blood cell. Sweat formed on the back of his neck, which turned ice-cold as the air conditioning blew around him. He watched the wings shudder in the strong wind and was acutely aware of his mother watching him. He felt anger rise in him, because he knew he couldn't just sneak a glance at her without her noticing, without her striking up a conversation. He had to watch the wings and the grey mass outside this box of metal.

"Are you okay, Will?" she asked. He wished he could roll his eyes at her.

"Yes." he answered, without turning his head.

She shifted in her seat and then let out a sigh loud enough for Will to hear it. He was sure that if she had any confidence that he would let her, she would have taken his hand. The flight from Bielefeld to Birmingham was less than two hours, but already, mere minutes after take-off, he wished his mother had left for home instead of coming with him.

Alex was waiting for him after all.

2

Standing at the window, Alex breathed in the smell of cleaning fluid. The skin on his hands felt raw and stretched, the chemicals seemingly having drained all life out of them. His stomach was growling; he hadn't dared eat lunch after cleaning the kitchen and putting everything where it belonged. He had even sorted through the herbs and alphabetised them again, the way Will liked it.

He knew Will would think this cleanliness and orderliness weird, perhaps even offensive. Alex had never before cleaned the house this meticulously just because Will came home. Secretly, he liked Will's little quips about the 'mess' he had let the house get into during Will's absence. They had the typical arguments about who was going to take the trash out, why the bloody remote control wasn't on the TV where they could easily find it or why last night's briefs were on the bathroom floor and not in the laundry basket. If he left dishes in the sink, Will cleaned them up; if dust was gathering in the hallway, Will was the one to get out the vacuum. But today, he simply hadn't been able to stop himself, had needed something to do. Alex looked around, realising how 'too clean and orderly' everything looked. He sighed and walked over to the TV, took the remote control and threw it on the couch where it fell in between two pillows, gliding smoothly into the downy depths and nearly disappearing completely.

He rolled his eyes, a small groan escaping his lips and went to retrieve it again, digging up an old tissue along the way. The phone rang just as he put the remote control back on the TV.

"Yeah?"

"How's your inner panic master doing? Has he outed himself yet?"

"I'm fine, Ruth. Thank you for asking." Alex sat down on the couch, rubbing a palm across his face. He wasn't sure whether he appreciated it or wanted to send Ruth to the hottest place in hell.

"Is the kitchen clean?" asked his sister.

"Yes."

"The living room?"

"Yes."

"Remote control?"

"On the TV."

"Bed made? Dirty laundry put away?"

"Yes and even washed."

"Did you clean the toilet?"

"Yes."

"Liar."

"I cleaned the toilet."

"No, 'liar' in answer to your 'I'm fine, Ruth'," she said in a mocking voice. "Liar!"

Since getting up from a restless sleep six hours earlier, he'd cleaned and sorted everything, read 35 pages of a book that didn't actually really interest him, watched the morning show, made five cups of coffee and finally repaired the squeaky chair that Will had been nagging about for...basically years. He could imagine a group of young psychology students standing about in the flat, scribbling away at all the fascinating signs Alex displayed and attempting a first-hand evaluation of his behaviour.

"It's still not too late for me to come with you. I can ditch the job for an afternoon. They won't mind," said Ruth.

Alex fought the urge to say yes. "Eleanor will be there. I have to go soon. We're still good for Sunday night?"

He could hear her hesitating on her end of the phone, but in the end she gave him the answer he wanted. "Yes. Seven sharp. I'll bring wine, okay?"

She hung up without waiting for an answer. He was grateful.

The remote control stared at him and he almost felt guilty for replacing it on top of the TV, because putting it back blatantly acknowledged that things weren't the same.

Getting up from the couch, he cast a last look around the living room. It looked too neat, and felt worse than on the day they had moved in. He went into the kitchen and retrieved his dirty coffee mug from the dishwasher. Placing the mug on the side table, he then unfolded the woollen blanket and just threw it across the couch. The remote control ended up next to the mug.

The kitchen in a way still looked like it wasn't theirs, but he ignored it, grabbed his jacket and left the house. He took a deep breath; the cold, stingy air he had felt this morning while taking out the rubbish had been warmed by the smell of lunch from the houses around him and the smell of grease coming from the pub kitchen at the end of the road. His stomach growled again.

He would have to eat lunch somewhere before driving to Clive Barracks.

3

His ears were beginning to ache from the 'thump thump' of the music. Ruth had vanished into the mass of bodies the moment they had stepped foot inside the club. Occasionally, he had seen her swaying by their corner table with some guy or other. Abby had tried to drag him onto the dance floor a little earlier, with less success than she had hoped for.

"Come on, Alex. Dance with me, let go a little. This is a great song."

So he'd danced that great song with as much enthusiasm as he could muster for a piece of music he didn't know from a genre he didn't really care for; and then escaped from Abby's wild hands towards the bar. A girl tried to talk to him there, but apart from the fact that he couldn't hear her, she also wasn't his type.

"Sorry."

He left her looking baffled and went towards the outside club lounge, hidden away in a small courtyard. Sweating bodies were swarming all over the big white sofas, splashing their drinks over the soft cushions. Everything looked misplaced inside the grey, cold enclosure. Alex went towards a dark bench at the back. A group of girls were watching him and he pointedly looked away.

A skinny guy narrowly walked past and sat down right next to him. Alex rolled his eyes and took another swig of his coke. His mood for conversation hadn't been great at the beginning of the evening and none of the events of the evening had helped to improve it. He slightly regretted agreeing to drive Abby and Ruth back home later. It could be hours before they wanted to leave.

"So who or what has bitten your arse?"

Alex looked to his right and saw the skinny guy staring at him with an amused grin on his lips. He was leaning forward with his arms on his knees, dressed in a shirt and jeans too large for his lean frame. A beer bottle was loosely hanging between index and middle finger. He didn't quite look like he belonged in this club either.

"Napoleon", answered Alex. It was his standard answer to stupid questions from pupils. During the first weeks, it made them laugh. After about two months, it shut them up without fail. When he said 'Napoleon' they knew they wouldn't get anything out of him. It had started out as a joke years ago, but he'd soon realised that it actually worked with all classes.

Skinny guy's eyebrows narrowed. "Napoleon?" He laughed. "I'm pretty sure, Napoleon wasn't tall enough to reach your arse."

"He was sitting on his horse," answered Alex.

"Sure it wasn't his horse that bit you?"

A very unattractive snort nearly made its way up Alex's throat, but he caught it in time. Instead, his hand came up to obviously hide his embarrassment by scratching his head. He risked another look and found the skinny guy staring right back at him. It should have felt strange, he should have been offended; got up and left. He should have been thinking: 'Great, of course I find the one gay guy in a straight club who also is a total freak. Just my luck.'

Loud laughter reached them from one of the sofas but neither bothered to look. Skinny guy even rolled his eyes, as if he wanted to say 'can you believe these people?'.

"So, your friends dragged you here too." Alex didn't even try to make it sound like a question. He suddenly felt as if they were on the same level, the same team, fighting against ignorant, snogging, salivating, drunk bodies.

"I must have had a temporary moment of insanity, because I actually offered to go with them and drive them home afterwards," answered the skinny guy.

"Welcome to the asylum. I have the same illness." Alex decided it was time to extend his hand and ask for skinny guy's name, but instead, he was nearly knocked over by a petite brunette, who stumbled on her high heels and only remained somewhat standing because she grabbed the back of his neck. He took a deep breath and managed not to shove her away hard and helped her stand up properly. She thanked him and proceeded to ogle his arms and chest and...

"I think you better look elsewhere for your one-night-stand." He grabbed her waist as gently as possible and turned her around. She wobbled a bit, but kept the balance, threw back her hair and stalked off. Well, stumbled off. Alex saw some drunk guys laughing at her from the other side of the courtyard.

"In your asylum, are you offering couple or single therapy?" asked the skinny guy and Alex tore his eyes away from the laughing jerks. There was a glint in the stranger's eyes that sent a shiver down Alex's back.

"Well, it's single therapy at the moment, but I'm willing to open up a space... sorry." Alex started laughing. He put his coke bottle on the ground. "That line sounded better in my head."

Skinny guy ducked his head and smiled. "My single or couple therapy-line wasn't exactly Oscar-worthy either." One of his hands ruffled through his hair, leaving it untidy. It looked good on him.

"It wasn't too bad. I'm Alex." The other's hand slipped into his; firm and strong with rough patches all over his skin.

"I'm Will." Their hands lingered a bit longer than was necessary or usual, but Alex was fascinated by the roughness of the skin. He thought Will was an office worker. He knew it was prejudiced, thinking that someone who was seemingly quite intelligent couldn't possibly be a blue collar worker. Sometimes, he surprised himself with how this sort of thinking snuck up on him. He could blame *his father and the way he raised his children, but that would be the easy way out and Alex hated that way. He preferred the detour of working on improving his behaviour.*

"Nice to meet you." They let go of each other, though Alex could have sworn that Will was sitting a little bit closer now. His beer bottle was still comfortably swinging between his fingers. By the looks of it, he had only had 3 or 4 swigs from it, as if he was just holding onto it to have something to do in this club.

"So, Will, what do you do that you need therapy?" asked Alex. "You know, while we're on the subject."

Will looked at his bottle, played with the label and took so long answering the question that Alex was already in the midst of mentally kicking himself. "Well, don't need it yet. But I probably will, some day." He shrugged as if to say it was alright. Or perhaps, Alex wondered, because he didn't quite know how to deal with a truth such as that. "Lance Corporal Will Collins, at your service. Or well, at the Queen's service." Will did a little bowing gesture. "And I won't be offended if you now think 'oh shit, a squaddie'. You have 30 seconds to leave this bench without me coming after you - starting now."

Alex grinned and slightly turned towards Will. "Alex Benson. History teacher. Wrote main thesis on miscommunication on front lines."

"How long was the thesis?"

"Pretty long."

"Thought so."

A comfortable and strangely familiar warmth spread through Alex as they both laughed; as Will ducked his head again as if he wanted to hide his amusement, as the smell of beer, oranges and something bitter that he couldn't quite make out engulfed him.

From the corner of his eye, he saw Ruth and Abby looking at him; looking at them.

*

"Name? Age? What does he do and by god, did you get his phone number?"

They had barely left the club and Ruth was already all over him, restricting his movement. It was hard to open the car door when your left arm was tortured by your sister. Alex sighed, a small white cloud forming in front of his mouth and immediately dispersing again. A cold wind was crawling around their colourful shapes, trying to draw them in. It bent the trees that stood along the road, forcing eerie creaking sounds out of them. They had to park a few minutes' walk away and after the loud chatter and overwhelming noises of the club, Alex relished the cold silence. As a child, he had always been amazed by the quietness snow brought with it, but also with how easily he could break it with his friends and their snowball fights.

Abby shivered and stepped a little closer to collect some of his body heat for herself. It woke him from his moment of dreaming, making him feel like Edmund coming home from Narnia. Except his adventure tonight had been a little more positive.

"His name is Will, don't know his age, he's a soldier and yes of course, I did. Though you seem to think I would be stupid enough to not get his number." Alex tore his arm away, shoving his sister towards the other side of the car a little too hard. She didn't mind, but instead turned around to her best friend.

"Abby, this is a historical moment. My brother, the obnoxious Alex, who thinks clubs are for sluts and twats, has scored in a club; making him either a slut or a twat. A lucky one though, because Will, no age, soldier with phone number, is fucking gorgeous!"

Abby giggled and coughed at the same time. She raised a shaky hand to high five with Ruth.

"I'm neither slut nor twat, and I'm pretty sure I never said that about clubs anyway," said Alex indignantly, as they climbed into the car.

"Ah, but you've thought it every time we went to one," said Abby. She reached around to put on the seatbelt, before putting both her arms around her chest. "Alex, it's freezing in here, turn up the heating."

Alex leaned over slightly and fumbled with the buttons. The car made sounds that he wouldn't have categorised as normal.

"The heating will soon come on," said Alex, though his voice did not convey reassurance.

"Get a new car," said Ruth while wiping the dashboard with her hands. "Seriously. You're on a teacher's salary, you should be able to afford a new car."

Alex scoffed, as did Abby. "As if a teacher's salary is enough to afford a brand new car," said Alex, starting the motor and looking in the side-view mirror. The air conditioning started blowing cold air into the car and Alex cursed under his breath. +

"It's not?"

"Not when you're single," said Abby, waggling her eyebrows at Alex. "Though a soldier probably doesn't get that much either."

"I only just met the guy, Abby," said Alex, rolling his eyes, but he couldn't hide a smile. Will was after all someone who'd managed to capture Alex's interest, which didn't happen very often, unless it was bratty 12-year-olds trying to graffiti the cafeteria.

"You know, you could always ask daddy dearest," said Ruth, while turning the knobs on the air conditioning.

Alex didn't turn his head, nor did he comment. He missed the significant look between his sister and Abby, though he knew it was there. It always was. The car slowly warmed up, more from their body heat than from the air-conditioning, and Alex pulled away from the parking space *and onto the road. He looked straight ahead, glad of his excuse to not have eye contact with Ruth.*

They drove home without a word, the only sound the luke-warm wind rushing out of the air conditioning.

4

Alex was waiting nervously, sitting in his now-fourteen year old Ford Escort, in front of the administration building at Clive Barracks. Alex would have liked it better if he'd been able to pick Will and Eleanor up from Birmingham airport, and he was sure so would they have. However, since Will was not to be admitted to the military ward at the Queen Elizabeth Hospital in Birmingham, he was obligated to sign in at his barracks as if he was a toddler gone rogue. 'Hey fellows, I played with guns and got blown up, but now I'm back, can I go home now with my mummy?' It seemed counterintuitive to force an injured man to report back to his military base.

But then, this had been Will's choice; there had never been the question of if he would go into military service, rather the question of when. A youthful fascination with military service and a hunt for historical immersions with his grandfather and dad had made it almost unavoidable that Will would become a recruit. His grandfather had been full of stories of World War I and II, of the Vietnam War, the Korean War, the Battle of Hastings, the Battle of Culloden. His knowledge of military history seemed never-ending, at least for Will. There was always another story that Will could listen to, a cup of tea in hand and a biscuit between his teeth. His grandfather could tell them as if he had actually been there and experienced it, though he never truly had. When Will told Alex that his grandfather had never actually served, Alex was shocked. It had been illness that prevented his recruitment; a true disappointment.

The summer before he died, they took his grandfather to Culloden. For Will, it was the third time. Alex remembered the awe that showed on Will's face, something Alex couldn't quite grasp standing in the middle of an untended field with nothing but grass and dirt in sight. For Will, it was a moment of solemnity, a kind of comfortable heaviness, and as he later said, a feeling of childhood and home. At that point in their relationship, he had already been out on deployment, but Alex remembered that moment on the field as the one when he truly acknowledged that he had fallen in love with someone who for lack of better words was meant to be a soldier.

Conversations around the topic had revealed an almost brutal recognition of possible consequences that Alex hadn't always felt quite comfortable with. Will was aware of things that could go wrong, was perhaps even more so aware of people's perceptions about overseas service, the media attention of the last decade about Iraq and Afghanistan and what he could expect in his future. It was a stoic and intelligently considered acceptance.

Alex avoided news segments about deployments, knowing it wouldn't help him worry less. He tried not to think about the situations Will would get himself into so he could sleep better at night. So he felt, it would have been better for Will if he had been able to go straight home. Who ever wanted to be reminded of the reasons why they got themselves into a bad situation?

He rubbed his eyes with the base of his palms.

He almost wished he could ask 'how did we get into this situation?' as if to shift the blame, but perhaps, it had been unavoidable and he should have prepared for this moment sooner.

He looked at the clock on the dashboard; it was getting close to two o'clock. He unclasped his seat belt and peeled himself from the old leather. Locking the car, he slowly strolled towards the main building. It wasn't busy, with most of the battalion still being in Afghanistan and only reservists and administration staff left to care for the compound. The few people he passed nodded at him, though he wasn't quite sure he remembered them. It wasn't in him to care and he knew that he was well known all over. It didn't matter how far the LGBT community had come in the last few years, a male military 'boyfriend' amidst all those military wives and girlfriends was still a rarity and Alex certainly was the only one here. At least the only one outed. You never knew.

The surrounding buildings were of Victorian standard; red brick, arched windows, pillars framing the entrances and smaller sections of the roof which stood out like castle turrets in the most clichéd medieval style one could think of. Some of the brickwork had chipped corners, almost as if there had been a stray bullet blasting away the brittle stone. The rain had faded the red in various places, or left dark, dank spots that would never go away, but overall it looked presentable. At least more so than the barracks Will usually lived in during the week, which looked like factory buildings. As if NCOs weren't already aware of their status as cannon fodder, chewed out on a conveyor belt to be put in front of bullets and bombs, not even worth the investment, used up and thrown away to be replaced by a new container. Alex hardly ever came near these buildings - Will was usually waiting for him somewhere near the car park - and he was thankful for it.

He passed through a heavy wooden door that had seen better days and registered with ever-smiling Private Johnson. "Alex Benson," although Private Johnson knew that. "Here to pick up Corporal Will Collins." Private Johnson probably guessed that one as well, but it was protocol and who was Alex to argue with military protocol.

Alex leaned on the counter, his jacket ruffling and his shoes screeching slightly. The ugly linoleum floor inside the buildings squeaked with every step. It was torn in places or had unidentifiable spots in some corners. The whole base needed to refurbish and repaint its interior, but money was never put into that. The grey linoleum floor and the egg-coloured walls remained, even though the linoleum couldn't necessarily be identified as grey anymore and the paint was peeling.

"How is he?" asked Johnson whilst typing in Alex's name.

Alex saw the sympathy in Johnson's eyes and with an unexpected urgency hoped that he wouldn't look like that upon seeing Will for the first time in 4 months.

"I don't actually really know. He's walking, that's all I know. Seeing him for the first time today."

The nauseous feeling from earlier that day came back and Alex pushed himself away from the counter, the squeaking linoleum making him wince. For some reason, it fitted his nervousness. The less he talked to anyone now, the better.

"Where can I wait for him?"

Johnson was capable of looking even more sympathetic - or pitying, Alex wasn't quite sure anymore - and even stood up from his chair.

"Well, he's over in C-Block for a conversation with Captain Malory, so you can go there or just wait in the car park, we don't mind," said Johnson. Despite his friendly behaviour and benevolent greeting Johnson was always following rules. He told you precisely where you could go and where you had to wait, and if you didn't do as you were told, he would personally throw you off the premises, or so Alex had been told. This lack of precision in Johnson's direction, therefore, for Alex translated to: 'You have earned the right to be wherever you want to be on this base.'

"Thanks." Alex tried to smile, but quickly gave up and walked away.

A little sun was peeping in through the clouds, making the cold air seem less threatening, though it would still be a few weeks until the rays of sunlight penetrated the skin as well as the sky, creating the warmth that everyone was craving. Alex's nose was starting to run, as it always did when exposed to freezing temperatures, and he took out a tissue as he walked across the concrete. C Block was a smaller though much more important building. The floors were covered with just the same ugly linoleum, but the ceilings were higher, the windows just a bit bigger and people carried themselves just a little taller, justified or not. Alex looked up at the rows of windows. Will would be sitting behind the windows in the top row on the right - Captain Anthony Malory's office. The windows reflected the sky and Alex assumed that he still wouldn't be able to see anything behind that glass, even if a person was standing directly at the window and looking down on him. He turned his back to the building and wondered whether he would ever be coming back here at all. From what people had told him, it looked as if Will's military career was over. Alex wasn't sure whether he would miss it, though he was sure that Will would.

"Getting killed is better than being injured."
"Why?"

This had been seven months into their relationship. His question had gone unanswered. Will had gotten up without a glance and gone into the kitchen, and Alex had known better than to pursue. It felt like 'death or injury' was the only major issue that they had ever disagreed on, however silent the disagreement may have been.

"I'm about to find out why," whispered Alex to himself. He sighed and kicked a pebble away from him, watching while it skitted across the concrete and vanished underneath a BMW. The hollow sound of pebble on concrete made Alex uncomfortable and the silence following it was unnerving. He checked to see if anyone was watching him, the disturber of the calm. A bird tweeted angrily from the branch of a nearby elm before setting off to somewhere more peaceful.

Alex put his hands in his jeans pockets and strolled along the edge of the car park, the toes of his shoes bending the grass and crushing it underneath the soles. He got out his phone, ignoring the multitudes of messages from his sister, Abby and Cohen and plenty of other friends. He couldn't deal with them just yet. He felt an element of satisfaction, having that power to release them all from their wonders and questions about Will's condition, about Will coming home. At least, there was this small familiar feeling he knew he must be sharing with Will at this precise moment, even if all else felt distant. Let them all wait; it wasn't for them to know yet; it wasn't for them to intrude – yet.

He distracted himself by scrolling through his Twitter feed, chuckling at Cohen's 6-Tweets-rant concerning the discontinuation of Cadbury's chocolate coins. It seemed they had always been the highlight of his Christmas stockings.

He didn't hear the door of C Block opening, nor did he hear the faltering of steps as he was spotted by two pairs of eyes. Instead Alex only turned around when he heard a bone-chilling cough tear through the air towards him, as if somebody's lungs desperately searched for something to hold onto because the body they were in wasn't suitable enough anymore.

Eleanor had her arm around Will's back, as he was bent over ever so slightly. His shoulders were tense, straining with the inner turmoil of wanting, but not daring to throw off the caring hand. His body was turned to the left and his head bent down, while he continued to cough into his hand.

Alex was glad he was allowed some time to get over the initial shock. He was glad he could spare Will from that first look of pity; the one he, Alex, had a minute to work on hiding. If he would have heard that kind of cough in school, that child would have been sent to the doctors or even the hospital without hesitation and with the biggest fuss.

'Breathe in,' demanded Alex silently.

17

Will stopped coughing, a wheezy drawing of air concluding his attack. Eleanor looked up, immediately found Alex. Even from the distance, Alex could see the worry lines across her forehead. He knew she allowed herself the same short moment as he had just done.

Lowering his hand away from his face, Will straightened up but before he'd turned towards him, Alex had already started walking towards C Block with a confident stride, trying to plaster a genuine smile on his face. A blunt bolt of lightning shot through his body as he saw Will's eye; as he saw the deep red bruising like make-up daubed across a fragile canvas, two healing scars that looked as if they were drifting away from the deep red and a white film covering the pupil like a diffusion filter on a camera lens. It was obvious on Will's face that he had seen the momentary shock and as they crushed together, Alex wasn't sure whether he was holding on so tight to comfort and reassure his boyfriend or whether he needed more time, just... more time. Nobody had told him anything. The coughing, yes, that was to be expected. He knew enough about chemical weapons to know that chlorine gas caused strong irritations to the lungs. Nobody had told him about the eye.

He suppressed the urge to take a deep breath, afraid it would make it seem like a chore to pull back and look at Will.

"Hi." Alex was conscious of trying hard to look into both eyes just as Will avoided his completely. One of his hands automatically wound itself upwards to lay across Will's neck, who looked up, eyes wide and searching Alex's face, recognising their little 'welcome home'-ritual: a family-friendly kiss while Alex's hand calmly rested at the back of his neck; the lips and the hand functioning as stabilisers.

The kiss was interrupted by another bout of painful-sounding coughs; a tanned hand clinging to his arm forcefully.

"Let's go home," suggested Eleanor and Alex nodded, even though all he wanted was to hug Will again.

Slowly, they made their way to his car.

5

It was quiet and lit up in a dark orange light by the sky and the street lamps when Alex stopped in front of their home. The road was winding its way up a low hill, whose top was hiding from view as the rough pavement curved to the left behind the rows of trees and houses lining it. The road was just wide enough for cars to park on either side, though larger vehicles rumbling up and down, every once in a while, had to navigate through tight spaces in case of oncoming cars.

Theirs was a small red brick house squeezed in between more equally small red brick houses, a dark green door with a rust-covered silver number 35 the only thing that made it stand out. Cohen had called it 'adorable, yet horribly conventional' and had ventured to ask them whether they really wanted to live there every time he came around; which was often. Not surprisingly though, Cohen soon had found the main advantage of this horribly conventional neighbourhood - the brewery just a few houses down the road, pub attached - and if there was one thing to appease Cohen, it was a beer brewery in the immediate vicinity.

Their house had a small front yard with two rhododendron bushes on each side of the door. Alex wasn't too fond of gardening and with Will gone most weeks of the year he had been the one to decide on the plants for their yard and garden out back. It was a given that he would pick plants that were easy to tend to. Still, the bushes were looking a bit sad, even for January and not for the first time, Alex thought he should have looked up how to tend to them during winter.

If it were up to Will, there would be flowerbeds to either side of their door and a thick but nevertheless well-tended jungle in the back garden with a variety of flowers, bushes and trees; with perhaps a small pond and a bank to sit on amidst the wild green. As it was, they only had a sickly looking birch tree, a gooseberry bush and a never-growing hedge. The only flowers finding their way into their garden were a few stray daffodils or crocuses in spring.

If you stood in the right place of the back garden, you had a slightly obscured, minimal, but nevertheless beautiful view of the river and the bank side park. It was Will's favourite spot, distinguishable at first by the patch of flat, yellowing grass and later by a smooth flat stone, much like a stepping stone, that Alex had put in for Will while he'd been away on his first tour in Kosovo. As most of the deployment involved capacity building, maintaining peace and aiding the locals, it was an easy first run. In comparison, Alex should have gotten him a brand new Ferrari as a welcome home gift this time.

Instead, he realised with a pang, he had nothing.

Alex turned off the ignition, the silence between them becoming more real. The streetlamp flickered. He glanced left and realised that Will's left hand hadn't left the door handle once since he'd gotten into the car. His right hand unbuckled the seatbelt in a well-known intuitive motion.

"Will, wait," said Eleanor sharply.

"What?"

"There's a car coming from behind."

Will's jaw tensed. "I know that, mum." Will looked ahead, eyes not even remotely flitting to one of the rear-view mirrors, ever the perfection of self-control that Alex had grown so familiar with.

Their relationship had often been a guessing game on Alex's part. It wasn't easy for Will to talk about feelings; as if it had been drilled out of him by the army. For Will, it had been easier to teach Alex how to read the signs.

So Alex got out of the car without a second glance to his side; pretending not to have seen Will's expression or pretending that things were as they used to be. He didn't care what Eleanor would think. This was a thing between Will and him.

He went around back to the car boot. A car door was slammed shut.

"You're going to have to park on the other side from now on, so that he can get out on the sidewalk," whispered Eleanor in his ear.

"Why?" He boldly stared at her and didn't bother to lower his voice. "All he has to do is turn his head far enough."

He slammed the boot shut. Will was now standing behind his mother. Their eyes met and for a moment Alex thought it was all going to be like it had been, but then Will bent down and lifted his duffle bag, a wheezing sound escaping his nose involuntarily. With sure strides Will walked past him and up to the front door. It would have seemed comical on any other day: Will walking up to the door with confidence, only to stop in front of, quite abruptly, because he remembered he would never get to his keys. He had his keys on him; he always took them with him on deployments. Alex thought it was sentiment, a feeling of home perhaps. A souvenir that took up space and collected dust, but was one of the most important things. However, it generally seemed to be a key's nature to slide into the deepest corner of any bag, never to be found again. Will would have had to spend ages to try and find his keys in the chaos of his duffle bag. Alex simply had to pull his out of his jacket pocket.

They awkwardly crammed into the small hallway, taking off their shoes and jackets. Will was leaning against the banister to the top floor, while he fumbled with his impossibly long laces. Alex was as in trance for a few seconds, standing by the still open entrance. Usually, Will went to the couch to sit down and untie these impossible boots and didn't get up from said couch till it was time to go to bed, following their routine of Alex happily providing him with food and drink for the rest of the evening. It was the kind of routine that made this house properly feel like home for Alex. The cold January air intensified the feeling of simply being a guest, as if this were only a short interlude before going to his real home. He shut the door, blocking out the cold, but it did not shut out this feeling of uncertainty. Trying to hide his confusion, Alex grabbed all the bags and brought them upstairs. Out of the corner of his eye, he saw Eleanor hovering by the door to the living room; visibly trying to restrain herself from mothering Will too much.

'It's not even been two hours and she's already failing,' thought Alex, as he put her bag on the guest bed. He hoped she wouldn't stay too long.

He entered the bedroom, putting Will's duffle bag on the queen-sized bed. He had perfectly made it up, changed the sheets and placed a glass of water on the right bedside table. Will always slept on the right side of the bed, straight on his back, with Alex curled up on the side to his left. More often than not, as the sun went up, Alex would shuffle closer to Will, slide an arm across his chest and Will would open his left eye to look at Alex – an acknowledgment that they were both semi-awake. If the corners of Will's mouth went up ever so slightly and his eyes glinted ever so mischievously, Alex knew he was in for some lazy or maybe not so lazy morning sex.

They wouldn't be able to do that anymore; Will wouldn't see him. He immediately realised it was a childish feeling, but he didn't want to miss out on all that. Perhaps, he should suggest that they switch sides?

"Leave it."

Alex jumped in surprise, looking over to where Will was leaning against the door frame. His hands had been lying on Will's duffle bag, playing with the zipper.

"Okay."

The lack of sunshine outside clouded Will in shadows and his expression was unreadable. Alex willed him to step forward, come into the room, approach him or at least shove Alex aside and start to unpack.

Alex was familiar with the little needles that had every now and again taken a wild stab at his heart every time Will was gone from their home. He had gotten used to them and was able to ignore them most times. But they were knives and chains now, twisting and turning inside and around his heart, crushing it. His fingertips tingled with a nervous anticipation that hadn't been fulfilled yet and a sour taste rose up to his mouth, making Alex swallow hard.

"Okay," he said again. He dropped his hands, letting them hang by his side uselessly. "You know I was hoping I could quickly go through your stuff for evidence of those military shenanigans that you refuse to talk about, even though I'm sure that they're happening. All this secrecy with you guys, no fun for us civilians." Alex laughed nervously and knew he should have stopped talking after the 'okay'. Will didn't move, just stared ahead, but Alex was sure he wasn't even really looking at him.

"Right, I'll start on the dinner. It's chicken with stuff, you know. Anyway, it's going to take like 30 minutes, so..." He paused, growing ever more desperate the longer he talked. He needed to suppress the sour taste again to keep himself from choking on his own words. "...well, take your time."

He stepped towards the door to leave the room and thought Will would move out of the way. Instead, he remained where he was, effectively blocking Alex's way out.

"Will?" asked Alex quietly, his brow furrowed and his heart beating wildly. He hated it when he couldn't predict Will.

"Can you-" Will leaned his head against the door frame. He closed his eyes, though Alex noticed that the eyelids on his left eye didn't fit together properly anymore. A small gap showed the milky whiteness behind them, a stark contrast to the bruised, fragile skin. The muscles around the eye twitched as if Will could feel the disruption and his hand was half-way to his face when his brain realised that scratching might be a bad idea. Alex wondered how painful it was.

"If you say: 'Can you sleep on the couch tonight?' forget it. Not going to happen. I did not just spend four months alone in that bed for you to kick me out of it the first night you're back," said Alex, involuntarily using his teacher voice. It always sounded ridiculous used on adults, never mind his own boyfriend, and Alex wasn't quite sure where those words in that voice had actually come from. "Sorry."

"No, it's fine." Even through the shadows and low light Alex could see the beginnings of the smile. The sour taste disappeared a little. "No, I wanted to ask...this sounds horrible, but can you get rid of my mother? I...um..."

"I'll talk to her."

Alex stepped closer, pulled Will away from the doorframe and got up on his toes. One arm snaked around Will's waist and the other around his shoulders. Alex placed a small kiss just underneath Will's eye before pulling him as close as he could. The tension in the broad shoulders did not dissipate, but at least, Will pulled his arms up to hug back.

"I'll get you when dinner is ready," said Alex and without looking at him again, he left for the kitchen.

6

Will sat down on the bed, looking out of the window down at their garden and the river in the distance. Two joggers were running along the river bank, disappearing again before Will could make out whether it was Mr and Mrs Lloyds from three houses down. He watched the ripples on the water, as the light around him slowly faded into an early January night. Despite the warmth of the house around him, Will shivered in the darkness. The sharp contours of the trees and houses that he could see through the window dissipated, leaving vague silhouettes, while the water in the river continued to glisten from the electric light of streetlamps. Will couldn't look at it for long, as the lights that were being thrown about by the multitudes of tiny waves made him feel sick. He lowered his head, focusing on the carpet. It felt far away, his brain not yet able to adjust to the shift in visualisation. As the room grew darker, the abyss under his feet grew more threatening. He could feel the carpet, but not see it. It made him nauseous, but he remained on the bed, clutching its side and continued to look down.

It was Alex who turned on the lights as he came to call for dinner, the light flooding his vision and his stomach cramping up as the memory raced through his mind. His hand instinctively shot up to cover his face and he flinched as his fingers touched the bruised skin.

Alex didn't comment on the still packed duffle bag. Will was relieved.

7

"The offer still stands, I could drive you down." Alex was hovering near Eleanor, hands in his pockets to shield them from the cold. It was a bad habit that he constantly forgot to take his gloves with him. His hands were cracked, little red lines all over where the skin had parted to let out droplets of blood. It would take Vaseline to heal them again.

"Don't be ridiculous. Don't waste your Sunday by driving up and down the country. I don't even have to change trains anywhere. And though I may be old, I'm still perfectly capable of getting on and off a train," said Eleanor. She was already paying for the ticket, fumbling with a crumpled 20 pound note that wouldn't go in the machine. "Besides, that way I can read."

Alex felt guilty at the sad tone in her voice. The little blue trolley bag beside her hadn't been unpacked. After a very late breakfast, she had simply gone upstairs closed the bag with a snap and carried it down. They had said goodbye and left the house within 20 minutes of that. Alex hoped she understood, though he wasn't sure he did.

The machine spat out the ticket and change and they moved away to make room for the next person. Alex was pulling the trolley up to the barrier. Eleanor took her time putting away her wallet, pulling her gloves up even though they hadn't slipped from her hands even a millimetre and straightening her coat. She smiled at Alex, but it was forced.

"Don't let him push you away."

Alex sighed and slightly shook his head. "He didn't-"

"I know, it's – I know. Don't worry about it." She placed a hand on his chest, pretending to smooth out his jacket. "I'll call you when I'm home and you call me when you need ... well, anything."

Alex leaned down to place a kiss on her cheek. "I will."

With one last brush across his jacket, she turned around and went through the barrier. She looked back quickly before she started to climb the stairs with her trolley, but did not linger. Alex felt like she should have slapped him and not kiss him on the cheek.

8

On his way home, he stopped by the Shrewsbury Market to get fresh supplies for dinner. It was a necessity for Alex to cook well, especially as Will mostly got MREs on tour, which provided the right nutrients, but not the right kind of pleasure you were supposed to get from food.

The market was packed, as usual, with people browsing for cooking ideas and cheap deals or eating their Sunday lunches at one of the stalls. The small chip shop at the entrance to the market was bursting; their chicken curry of the bone with chips an absolute favourite with locals. The smell of spices and coconut milk wafted over from the few Indian food stalls and mixing with the tantalising smells of a bakery. The sugary air would have lulled Alex into a comfortable and lazy warmth, had it not been for the cold January wind that gently blew through the market, intensifying the steam coming from all corners. The movement of the customers whirled up the steam, creating a mystic atmosphere. Alex walked past the Turkish man at the Kebab stand shouting for customers in his broken English. Alex greeted him; he was teaching his son. The vegetable stalls were at the other end of the market, past the ready meals and past the butcher's shops. By the time Alex had made it there and back his clothes smelled of grease, smoked meat and a hundred spices. He found he never really minded so much. He bought an apple tarte in the small French patisserie across the road, where he was greeted by what he presumed was another parent before heading home.

As he turned onto his street, he immediately noticed the dark green Audi A3 parked near his house, with its wobble head Doctor Who figure on the dashboard. He sighed and wished he hadn't taken the detour to the market.

There was a light in the living room but no voices coming from it and Alex already had the image in his head of Will and his sister silently sitting across from each other, Will staring at nothing, while Ruth tried to sneak glances at him. Alex took off his shoes and threw the jacket across the banister. He was ready to fire off some snarky remark, only to step into the living room and see Ruth lounging on the couch, reading a book with her legs elegantly draped across the cushions. Will was nowhere to be seen or heard.

"Wha-?" Alex's mouth hung slightly open in surprise

"Hello, dearest brother." Perhaps it was a sign of the gravity of the situation they were all in; it didn't leave room for jokes, or else, Alex would have been on the receiving end of one. He could see his own surprised face reflected in the dark TV and had to admit it looked comical. Ruth tended to be quick on sarcasm and cynicism when the situations arose, which usually involved her making fun of her brother. However, she simply put the book down on her lap and gave him a weak smile.

"Where's Will?" Alex took a quick look into the kitchen, but finding it empty, sat down in the armchair to the right of the couch. From that position, he could look out into the hallway, the banister half hidden from view. Ruth took her time putting in the bookmark and sorting out her slightly rumpled dress. Keeping up pretence was her favourite pastime when she was as worried as Alex. She still did it even though they both knew that Alex had found out about her tactics years ago.

"Well." She drew the word out; another tactic of hers, trying to give herself time to think about the ways the ensuing conversation might play out. "He let me in, sat down with me for about two and a half minutes and then he got up and disappeared upstairs." Ruth continued combing down her dress, not looking up.

Alex rolled his eyes and stood up again, ready to go upstairs. "What did you say to him?"

Ruth grabbed his wrist to stop him. Her feet were on the floor now and she looked up at him. "I swear, Alex, all I said was hi and it looked like everything was fine, but he never said anything in return and then he disappeared upstairs. I've just been sitting here since, reading this slightly boring book." She folded over the corner of the page she was on before closing the book. "Honestly, for a second I thought he'd gone deaf, but I kept thinking you would have called me last night and warned me."

She reached out with her hand, waving it gently to make him sit down. Alex allowed his sister to pull him down beside her.

"He's not deaf. And besides, why should I warn you when you're not even supposed to be here yet, you know, without me around," he said.

"It's Sunday. We had a dinner date for Sunday." Ruth folded her arms across her chest; a gesture she loved using when trying to make a point. She'd always been intrigued by the distant aura it gave her and the stumbling incoherency it produced in others. Standing tall, her long dark hair flowing over her shoulders, her sharp eyes glaring and her arms folded she could argue her way out of a situation with absolute confidence. She had been able to get away with anything and he had always lost every argument with her. In the long run, however, it had helped him in classrooms so many times. Students liked to try their best to persuade teachers to watch a movie or do something 'fun', or else they tried to argue against him in an attempt to prove him wrong. He had yet to lose those kinds of arguments. No one was as convincing as his sister; most of the older students in his classes had stopped trying.

"Dinner being the operative word. We said seven sharp," said Alex, looking at his sister with raised eyebrows.

"I'm just a little bit early."

"It's three o'clock."

"Your clocks are clearly wrong."

Alex sighed deeply and leaned back, closing his eyes. Ruth folded up her legs and let her head fall onto his shoulders.

"I wanted to see him, make sure he's really here." She whispered the last part and Alex almost didn't hear it.

"He's different," whispered Alex in return.

Ruth raised her head again and looked at him, affronted. "Did you expect him to be exactly the same?"

"No, I – obviously not, but- It's just-" Alex put his head in his hands.

"This would be a good time to finish at least one sentence you started."

"He barely talks. He's said three sentences to me and he made me put his mum on a train home, Ruth," said Alex, still whispering.

"Did you sleep in the same bed?"

Alex nodded.

Alex had called him down just before he had taken the chicken out of the oven. It had been another five minutes before Will finally came down. The food had been plated up and steaming away on the table. Eleanor had been sitting with her back to the window, glancing towards the door every few seconds until Will had walked through it. It had seemed to pacify her that at least he was eating with them, but Alex had wondered for how long exactly Will had contemplated not coming down at all. Alex had tried to strike up a conversation, asking about the flight, the hospital, anything he needed to know, all the while carefully watching Will. Watching a Will who never answered, who ate faster than normally and drank large gulps of water after every other bite. Alex had been able to see Will's jaws and throat working and knew that Will was trying to hide a raw throat and stop himself from coughing. It was calculation, it was to help Alex persuade Eleanor to leave the next morning. Alex had also noticed that Will wasn't looking at either of them throughout the meal. As soon as his knife and fork had clanged onto the empty plate, Will had taken to staring at the water jug, as if willing it to fill up again.

"I do like what you have done with the house," Eleanor had said at some point, pointedly looking around at the barely changed kitchen. There was simply a new mixer on the counter. It had been a while since she'd been here, but Alex had nevertheless felt it to be a poorly concealed attempt at getting Will to comment on something. There hadn't been any changes. Alex hadn't had the time to make any. And Will knew that. Alex's eyes had flickered to Will to see his reaction, but nothing had shown on his face.

"Thanks, Eleanor. It is a nice house. It was already nice when we got it."

"I know, but still. It's nice." Her voice had drifted off slightly, realising the fruitlessness of her efforts. She had lowered her eyes and it had looked like the weight of the world had been pressing down on her shoulder. He had found it heartbreaking and the only reason he hadn't reached out towards her hand had been his insecurity as to what Will would say to that.

After the chicken dinner, Will had gone up straight away. He had slowly walked into the dark corridor, not switching on the light as he moved up the stairs as if he were trying to get used to the darkness. Alex had done his best to make Eleanor understand why her son wanted her to leave, but he could tell she was upset and unwilling. She had left him, agreeing that she would go after breakfast, but he had still felt uncomfortable. He had slowly finished his beer in semi-darkness, the only light the small lamp in the corner of the dining room, the only noise his own pulse.

It had been past midnight when he'd gone up to bed. Will was wheezing in his sleep, chest rising and falling irregularly. The wheezing had given him the urge to wake

Will up and drag him to the hospital. He undressed as quietly as possible, simply throwing the clothes on top of the dresser, and brushed his teeth in darkness. The light of the ensuite bathroom caused a similar kind of brightness in the bedroom as the morning sun would, even through the narrow cracks of a closed bathroom door, and Alex didn't want to wake Will up. He had slipped into bed with the least amount of motion he could muster. One of his hands had inched closer to Will's shoulder, just to touch him, in a way to make sure he was there. Will had flinched, out of instinct Alex assumed, so the hand had retreated but stayed close to the shoulder all night. In the morning, however, it had lain on an empty side of the bed.

"Doesn't mean it also felt that way," said Alex in answer to Ruth's question.

"Well, yes alright, but at least he didn't kick you out?" Ruth said.

Alex sighed. "Only because I wouldn't let him."

A smile began to grow on Ruth's face. "See, there you go. Tough army guy but he still takes shit from you. Because he loves you."

"I never disputed that." Alex got up to go into the kitchen and jerked his head at Ruth to follow him. She looked around at the soft couch, as if reluctant, but she also knew that they couldn't have this conversation in screaming voices when Will was right upstairs possibly hearing everything.

"Then give it time," she said, untangling her legs from underneath herself. "Do we really know what happened?"

"No, I wasn't really told that much. Didn't even know about his-" Alex stopped mid-sentence and Ruth nearly ran into him.

Will was sitting at the kitchen table, playing with the ends of a napkin. His bad eye was facing the other way and Alex wondered whether Will had sat down that way on purpose even though his usual seat was opposite. Quite when he had come downstairs, Alex couldn't say, and it unnerved him that Will was sneaking around in such a way. They had two entrances to the kitchen and dining area, one from the hallway and the other, larger double door entrance, from the living room. Originally he had found the two separate entrances nice, but he was slowly changing his mind. He would never know when exactly Will had snuck into the kitchen via the hallway and how much he really had heard.

"They wouldn't let me call you. They thought any talking would worsen my condition." Will's voice was low, but clear. He looked at the napkin in his hands, small crumbs all over it.

Ruth dug her elbow in Alex's side and he returned her proud 'See I told you so'- smile with a 'Yes you were right'-roll of his eyes.

"It's okay," he said to Will with a distinct shrug of his shoulders. It was their code for 'I know you're lying and we really need to talk about this when we're alone'.

9

Alex used to hate cooking, mostly because cooking in their household meant putting ready meals into microwaves or ovens and always reminded him of how little time his own father was willing to spend with his family. He'd seen classmates cook meals with their entire family crammed into their tiny kitchen. Someone else's mum had tried teaching him how to cut vegetables correctly or how to do a good stew. Explanations about the right amount of herbs and salt and pepper ringing in his ear, trying to enter his long term memory, followed closely by his promise to try this at home. It had always been nice and enjoyable, but once he'd reached his own home, the rush of happiness disappeared again. Gone was the information, gone was the promise. All he'd ever done at home that resembled cooking was stirring the tinned soup in the pot while heating it up, or him and Ruth making toast together in the mornings. All he ever associated with the kitchen were clean white tiles, a smell of cold distance and the whiskey glass he would find by the sink nearly every morning.

Will had laughed at him once he'd found out that Alex wasn't only so much as inexperienced in cooking but was also really rather awful at it. Although aware of the physics in itself, Alex had needed three tries in order to finally make decent spaghettis that had not been slowly turned into charcoal. It took him a few months before he really got into it and started trying out more and more recipes.

It had taken about two years, however, for Ruth to stop laughing whenever she saw Alex in a kitchen preparing food. She still survived on microwave meals or take-out, but eventually accepted her brother had moved on. She'd even given him a new set of knives for Christmas – in all colours of the rainbow of course and with a card that said 'Who am I to deny your domestic tendencies? Love you'.

It turned out that Will wasn't the new Jamie Oliver either. His steak was half-decent and he managed to do pasta and the usual simple basics, but Will was never really one to rush to the kitchen when it came to the question 'Who's cooking dinner tonight?' He, having been fed artificially produced MREs for most of his adult life, was rather quite fond of the idea of Alex cooking for him. So very early on in their living-together stage, they'd established certain roles, as clichéd as it sounded. Alex was the cook and bed-maker. Will was the gardener, plumber, carpenter and thief-thwarter. He'd pointed out to Will how unfair that setting was, but he'd only gotten a shrug in return – and a blowjob; the first of many indications that Will was really rather turned on by food and cooking. It was quite the incentive for Alex to establish his cooking skills.

They were still cutting the ingredients when the doorbell rang for the first time, an hour before the set time of 7pm. Alex rolled his eyes, dried off his hands on a paper towel and went to open the door.

"Hey!!! I know I'm early, but it was so boring at home and-"

"Save it, Cohen. Ruth's been here since three," interrupted Alex, quickly hugging Cohen with one arm.

"Oh wow. Ruth early? That's a new one. I brought wine. Where is he?" Cohen shoved three bottles into Alex's arms before throwing his jacket over the banister.

"Kitchen." Cohen rushed past him, opening his arms wide as he stepped through the kitchen door.

"Will! My friend! Nice to see you actually still have all your limbs." There was a scraping of chairs, a clinking of glasses and cutlery on plates meaning that Cohen had bumped into the table in his haste to hug his best friend.

Alex re-entered the kitchen and over Cohen's shoulder, Will looked at him with a question on his face. *Did you tell him?* Alex ignored the accusatory look and put the wine on the table before going back to cutting up the peppers.

"Cohen, if you don't let go soon, you will have crushed him to mousse," remarked Ruth, a playful smile on her lips.

"You're just jealous I'm not feeling you up all over." He finally let go, taking a step back to look at Will. "You know, if you pull it off well enough, you can scare the living shite out of these Taylor kids from down the street."

"Oh my God, Cohen!" Ruth put her knife down and stared at Cohen with a shocked, yet amused expression. Alex stayed quiet, waiting for Will to react.

"What? I'm literally stating the obvious here." Cohen studied Will's face. "These scars around the edge are still healing right?"

Will cleared his throat. "Yeah."

"Pity. Looks scary cool."

The problem with Cohen, as Alex had slowly discovered, wasn't that he didn't know when to stop; it was rather that you were never sure whether he needed to stop at all. He had a knack for saying inappropriate things in a charming way that made you accept and possibly even respect him more than it made you dislike him. And once you got past the hidden insults, as Will had almost decades ago, his comments were mostly amusing. Only Cohen was able to get away with them.

Cohen sat down and he and Ruth immediately started chatting, and inadvertently flirting as usual. However, Will remained quiet most of the time, drinking his tea and reacting only half-heartedly. If it was awkward for them, neither Cohen nor Ruth let on.

By the time, Abby and Matt arrived, Will already looked exhausted from trying hard to control his lungs and his reactions. He was too polite to disappear again as he had done with Ruth, but Alex felt the tension emanating from Will's every cell.

Sitting around the dinner table, drinking wine and waiting for the shepherd's pie to be cooked, Alex noticed Will fidgeting with a napkin again, as he'd done earlier that day. The conversation was going on around him, but he didn't participate. He coughed every now and again, looking around to see if anyone paid attention to that. Abby sometimes couldn't hide her worried frown but she did her best to put on a cheerful mask. Matt threw nervous glances at Alex, who didn't know how to react to them. Ultimately, it was Ruth and Cohen who were the best at pretending, always had been.

Will barely drank, swirling the wine in the glass rather than consuming it, continuously clearing his throat as quietly as possible, while everyone else chatted away about work and family and life in the way Will has always asked them to: 'Pretend I've never been away.' Usually he and Will would entangle their feet at some point during dinner, but Alex was too anxious to make the first move. One jerk of Will's knee away from him, a frown forming on Will's face and it would become harder to pretend. Alex hoped Will would relax more with the wine and the company that he liked best.

"To Will," said Cohen suddenly, raising his glass. For once, he didn't add anything and Alex was glad. The others repeated the call and drank, however, once the glasses were sat down again, Will excused himself.

Silence followed, as they all listened to Will climbing the stairs despite the fact that there was a guest toilet on the ground floor. Alex knew why he'd gone upstairs and thought it was stupid of Will to think they wouldn't hear. Abby let out a sigh releasing the tension that Alex felt like echoing. And then gut-wrenching sounds tore up the silence. It seemed worse now that Will had spent the entire evening trying to swallow his coughs; as if his lungs were now breaking out of their imprisonment and needed to make up for lost time.

"Tell me that's a cold!" said Cohen, eyes wide. Alex didn't answer. "Fucking hell, is he going to have that for the rest of his life?"

"I don't know," said Alex quietly. Abby's hand stretched across the table to cover his, squeezing lightly.

"He might not," she said with what she probably thought was a soothing voice. It worked on her pupils, but was not as successful when she wasn't quite so calm herself. "I mean it hasn't been that long since the accident, maybe it'll get better over time with medication. He's got an inhaler right?"

"Yeah."

"So it will probably improve." Abby looked up at the ceiling as she said this, the sounds making their way downstairs not helping her argument.

The timer on the oven went off and Alex extracted his hands. Any excuse to get busy was welcome. Ruth got up as well. Growing up in the Benson household should have been good practice for awkward situations, but in fact, it had only made them more sensitive to them and always eager to get away.

Will came back into the room and sat back down without really looking at anyone. Alex ducked down to open the oven and take of care of the pie, acutely aware of the otherwise silent room. He heard the scraping of a chair and looked up to see Cohen leave the kitchen and go upstairs, closely followed by the sound of a door being opened and a lot of rummaging through cupboards and drawers.

"Cohen! Can we help you with something?" yelled Alex upstairs, hot shepherd's pie in his hands ready to be placed on the table.

"I'll be down in a minute."

Ruth and Matt shrugged roughly at the same time, which was almost comical.

"You could always say he won't get any food if he doesn't stop immediately," suggested Matt, a rather resigned look about him. When Cohen was setting his mind to something, it took four bottles of vodka, a tank and five blondes to stop him – in that order, he had to be slowed down first to notice the blondes after all.

Ruth motioned for Alex to finally put down the pie and was already starting to put some of it on Abby's plate, when they finally heard Cohen stomping back down. He sat down without saying something, raised his closed fist and carefully put down the inhaler in front of Will's plate. The others all stopped for a minute, watching the inhaler or watching Will. Finally, Will almost unnoticeably nodded at Cohen and held up his plate for Ruth to put pie on it.

When he thought it would go undetected by Will, Alex mouthed 'Thank you' at Cohen.

10

His left eye was tearing up – another grain of sand stuck underneath his eyelid. He blinked repeatedly and wished he could reach up with his hands and rub the grain out. But it was hands on rifle and full attention. It felt like sand and gravel was everywhere, scratching at his body in all the odd places, even though he knew that couldn't possibly be. In order to keep out any chemicals from a gas attack, the hazmat suit was designed as a closed-circuit, nothing could enter, nothing could get out. His sweat was circulating around it in a never-ending race of salty droplets. Yet, he couldn't shake the feeling of itchiness. He rubbed his back on the leather of his passenger seat, the rifle never swaying from its position out of the window, his eyes never straying from his one to three o'clock cover zone. Not that there was anything suspicious to be seen. His eyes fell on a flat, sandy horizon with not a bushel to hide behind or a hole to crawl into. Anything he couldn't see coming here, he would never see coming.

He sighed. Sometimes, he wished he could see Afghanistan without a helmet, a hazmat suit, an Ocelot and most importantly, a rifle. He imagined the night sky in this part of the country would be incredible. No artificial light to disturb it. They rarely stayed in one place long enough or at decent enough hours to truly enjoy their surroundings, and when it was 25% sleeping, 75% alert, you made the best of your allocated sleeping time and didn't think twice to waste it by looking at stars. The only constant they had, had been Koh-i-Baba and the impressive extensions of the Hindu Kush. He'd told Alex about the incredible mountain ranges in his emails, but any words he had found to describe them were only a fraction of the original beauty. He had managed to take a few photos of the high peaks in the early hours of the day and sent them across to Alex and his mum. They were awe-inspiring and grounding at the same time. The mountain range itself was thoroughly unimpressed with the war that was raging at its feet, eating and reflecting the sunlight with each day that the conflict continued. They were not going to move, standing steadfast in their little spot of earth while the silly, little humans fought over the land below, perhaps because of the treasures within those mountains, or not. No one really knew, not many had the energy to care. It was orders here and orders there and that was what you did anyway.

A burnt-out truck began to appear on the horizon at the 12:30 position. There was no smoke billowing from it, the only heat rising from it was the heat of the sand. Will concentrated on the metal ruin, narrowing his eyes. It was a perfect hide-out.

Andrew to his left was saying something, yelling something, but he couldn't hear it, could only see the hand gestures from out of the corner of his eyes. He laughed nonetheless and didn't know why. His brow furrowed and he blinked. The grain of sand was still lodged behind his eye-lid. He swore. The Ocelot hit a small bump and suddenly jerked up, turning everything upside down. He blinked again.

One. The sun was burning his eyes.

Two. His helmet rattled.

Three. An explosion shook the Ocelot, a flash blinding him. He shut his eyes tight and his hand loosened from his rifle for a few seconds before he regained control of his senses and gripped it tight. He needed his rifle.

Smoke was billowing up into the sky on their right, obscuring the view of the terrain. Andrew was shouting at him and Leon was firing off rounds into nothingness, a dull thud echoing inside his head. Will pulled up his weapon, looked around, then stopped.

His eyes were bloodshot, his clothes ragged and torn and his chest fell and rose heavily. His fingers were on the trigger.

11

His eyes flew open, his blood racing through his veins. For a second he didn't know where he was. The room around him was dark, a low light coming in through the window that he barely registered. The duvet lay crumbled at his feet and the sheets were clinging to his sweaty back. He pressed the heels of his hands into his eyes, ignoring the sharp sting from the bruise. His breathing was irregular, his lungs aching with exertion. His heart was beating heavily, as if it tried to drum him apart from the inside, one layer of muscle and sinew crumbling away with each beat. He tried to swallow, but his mouth, his entire body felt dry, full of sand and gravel. Cold fingers touched his arm from out of the darkness. It stung his skin like a bullet and instinct took over. He grabbed the arm and pushed against the body with his full weight, twisting bones and pressing against muscles.

He heard the outcry of pain, but didn't quite register it as meaningful. It was Alex's blonde hair slightly gleaming in the low light that brought him back to his senses, focussed his mind and relaxed his muscles.

"Oh god, oh god, oh god." He let go of the hand that he had twisted and scrambled out of bed. He slid to the floor clumsily, his knees scraping over the carpet. The pain in his lungs increased, piercing his insides. Trying to draw breath he only coughed and leaned over, his head nearly bumping against the bedside table. His fingers scraped along the carpet, searching for something to hold on. The moonlight was creating a grey sea that he was prepared to drown in. The blurred waves seemed to encompass every particle around him and draw him in with every miserable breath. He heard the rustle of the sheets and felt the weight of a body next to him, and for a moment thought it would be someone to hold him down so he would drown faster. The voice that called him seemed far away.

"Will, WILL! Hey, hey, calm down, please calm down. It's fine, I'm fine, everything's fine. You're safe. You're in England. You're home." Alex grabbed Will by the neck, kissing his temple while trying to sit him up straight.

"Alex, I-" His own voice was barely audible, throat raw and not enough air in his lungs.

"Shit, shit, fuck, no breathe, please Will, breathe. Please calm down. Where's your inhaler thingy?" Alex's hands were shaking as they stroked Will's hair and his voice had the tone of panic. Somehow, it calmed him; the moonlight became sharper, the carpet became rougher under his fingers. Strong hands grabbed him by the shoulders and pulled his upper body towards the bed, leaning him against the soft mattress.

"Wait here," Alex got up, turned on the light and began to pull open the drawers, fumbling around in them fruitlessly. Will watched his reflection in the window, his chest heaving. "Where the fuck is it? FUCK! Stay here and...and breathe." He ran into the bathroom, opening cupboards, pulling their contents to the floor, eyes roaming wildly. It wasn't there and in frustration, he kicked the laundry basket, sending it across the room.

He saw the hesitation, the question in Alex's eyes whether to stay to calm him down further or leave him completely alone, even if for just a few seconds. Clutching his chest, he simply stared at Alex blankly, who turned and almost ran out of the room.

"Fuck, fuck, fuck!" He could hear Alex stumbling on the stairs and a dull thud as if he had run into the wall opposite the stairs. A light was turned on downstairs, a small glimmer in the dark house. There was another thud and an annoyed outcry of pain, before the light was switched off again. He could hear Alex taking two steps at a time, before bursting into the bedroom. Alex's chest was heaving as much as his, as Alex rushed over and shoved the inhaler in his mouth. His lungs seemed to be unable to decide whether to cough or wheeze, the medicine only slowly making its way to the bronchi. Will clung to it with wide eyes and white knuckles.

It felt like hours even though the clock had only moved from 2:13 to 2:15 by the time Will was calm again. His lungs were still wheezing, but the coughing had stopped. Tears were staining his face, a rare sight that made Alex damn that stupid white phosphorus grenade to hell. He sat down cross-legged, putting a steadying hand on the back of Will's neck.

"Why the fuck do you only have one inhaler?" said Alex, sounding himself as if he'd just run a marathon.

Will snorted, lips turning up into the first smile since coming back.

"And while we're on the topic, why the fuck did you leave it in the kitchen?" Alex said it lightly, meaning it to be a joke, but Will's smile vanished instantly.

"My lungs got permanently damaged only one and a half weeks ago. Excuse me that I'm not used to it yet." He looked away angrily.

"I...I know. I didn't-"

"Forget it. I'm better, I'm fine." Will shakily stood up, still leaning against the window. Alex followed him, careful not to place any weight on his right hand. It wasn't broken, but the pain that was snaking up his arm in waves told him that he'd need an ice pack nonetheless. He wasn't going to tell Will though. Alex was standing behind Will, close enough to touch, but didn't dare to. Will's hunched shoulders were an unpleasant sight.

"What did you dream about?" he asked, instead.

"Nothing," answered Will quietly, averting his eyes. He stepped around Alex and climbed back into bed. Alex stared at his own reflection in the window, hoping Will would say something else. There was still that elephant in the room from earlier, when he'd lied to his face in Ruth's presence.

When silence persisted, he turned and went towards the door. "I'm gonna get a glass of water. And tomorrow. we're getting more inhalers. We can't do this every night."

If Will wondered why Alex took half an hour for a glass of water, he never indicated it. Alex, however, noticed that the bedside lamp was still on when he returned to the bedroom; Will sound asleep again, his chest continuously wheezing in an irregular rhythm.

12

Still sleeping at six in the morning, Will looked peaceful for the first time since returning and Alex stayed in bed for another 15 minutes, just looking at him. Will had his faced turned towards the left, his injured eye half-hidden in the pillow, darkness swallowing the evidence of it. The skin glistened slightly in the dim moonlight shining through the window. His chest was rising and falling slowly, the low wheezing sound the only evidence that not everything was normal. Alex had the urge to put his hand on Will's chest to feel the air reach every corner of his lungs, filling it up to the brim and letting go again, exhaling every bad gas it contained. He restrained himself, just sighed and let his eyes roam over face and chest. Will seemed so far away. The same person in a different world. Alex slowly and quietly got up, more to distract himself than because he wanted to. His job was waiting, his kids were waiting, and his lesson preps were most definitely waiting.

Once he got to school, remembering the long Monday ahead, any feeling of peace had completely dissipated. Mondays were hell – full schedule without a free lesson in between, plus more often than not, staff meetings in the afternoon.

A few students were sitting on the steps to the main entrance, huddled together for warmth, possibly getting a bladder infection from the cold, concrete steps, but nevertheless, unwilling to go inside the dreaded building sooner than they would have to. They were blowing billows of steam out of their mouths, which was impressive in light of the lack of cigarettes in their hands. One of the girls wore a thin coat, a skirt and tights, shivering into her boyfriend's shoulders. He did often wonder whatever made them think that these clothes were appropriate for a cold January morning. He himself wore a coat he'd bought in Canada and he was cold.

Alex walked past them with a quick, mumbled greeting, receiving a similar one in return.

Stepping through the door, he saw a Sixth Former just waiting in the reception. "Good morning, sir."

"Morning, Gareth."

Gareth came from one of the outside villages, the ones with tiny roads winding through them that made you think you could not come out of this without a metal collision. Massive busses navigated around the area and brought around a third of their pupils to their school. Gareth's bus needed to do two tours and usually arrived almost 45 minutes before school started, giving him plenty of time to kill and making him a well-known face among the teachers. He was one of Alex's favourite students. Not that you were supposed to have favourites as a teacher, but you did anyway. Gareth was from a large farm that struggled to keep up with modern economy. Gareth had early on realised that he did not see farm life in his future and had struggled with his father's wish for him to take over the business until Year 11. Alex remembered the long conversations that had kept him occupied for months. Perhaps it was that sense that a life suppressed isn't a good life, a sense that Alex was only too familiar with. It made him fight for Gareth, almost as if he was his own son. Gareth's father, of course, regretted Gareth's decision to do A-Levels in History, English, Philosophy and German, but eventually accepted his son's wish. As far as Alex knew, they had an understanding.

"Sir?" Gareth walked beside him, away from the classroom he was supposed to have his first lesson in and towards the Humanities office.

"Yes, Gareth?" Alex turned the key and opened the door slightly too forcefully, slamming it into the wall. The door handle dug itself deeper into the wall. There was already a small hole and plaster hanging loose as just about everyone in the office had the same tendency of opening the door with a certain amount of force. With 20 students around you asking for this homework, begging to be let off this detention or participating in a fruitless attempt to get test scores or perhaps even test questions out of them, and all of that in those ten minutes of break you may have between lessons, no one really had time to worry about a stupid door and a stupid wall. When the janitor and site team complained, the common response was to say that they should have designed the walls better. Or installed a little doorstopper in the floor before their door-slamming ripped out more of the plaster. No one ever installed anything.

The office was an organised mess. Shelves lined the walls and groaned under the weight of paper, books, DVDs, games and general stationery. All of their desks were hidden underneath more paper, mostly exams, and an assortment of different coloured pens, paper clips and folders. There was leftover cake on the far side of the room that Martha had brought in on Friday and not taken home. He'd meant to take a piece before he left for the weekend, but had eventually forgotten all about it. It looked rancid and dry now. He dropped his bag by his chair and sat down, nudging the mouse of his computer to wake it up, before taking off his jacket.

"What is it Gareth?" he looked up, perplexed as to why the boy hadn't spoken yet. He had a sheepish look on his face and was lingering by the door. Alex wondered whether Gareth had forgotten the homework, and more so, whether he should be disappointed about it. He found he didn't care so much today. The computer came to life and Alex started putting in his password.

"If you don't mind me asking, but how is Mr. Collins?"

Alex stopped in his tracks, hands hovering above the keyboard, and looked at Gareth in surprise. He had expected his students to find out about his relationship with Will at some point, but he had also expected to be acutely aware of their knowledge. He had often made speeches in his head, depending on possible scenarios where it might become appropriate or perhaps necessary to divulge information about his personal life. And it seemed, he needn't have bothered. He did not recall a moment when students may have been whispering about a rumour, when one even may have been brave enough to ask. He did not recall any mention of having been seen in town with Will. However, not only did they seem to know he was gay, they also seemed to know about Will's profession and accident, and Alex simply wondered how and since when.

"He's..um..he's fine. Wounded, but alive and walking. Thank you."

Gareth nodded. "There was an article in the Chronicle, just a small one, saying that Corporal Collins was wounded in action."

"Really?" Alex frowned. "What else does it say?"

Gareth shrugged. "Nothing much... Nothing about you."

Alex raised his eyebrows. It almost felt like he wasn't part of the conversation, simply an observer, a TV audience about to be surprised with a big revelation. "How do you know? How does anyone know?"

Gareth, to his credit, blushed. "I'm not sure many people know, but I saw you walking near the army compound one day, and you know, my uncle works there too and I asked him and he ... yeah, he told me." He paused, waiting for a response from Alex, perhaps afraid Alex would get angry. "But, I never told anyone else, so, yeah, I don't think anyone really knows. Not that it matters, sir."

Alex looked away, his father's cold eyes flashing in his mind, the passer-by's spit on the tip of his shoe in a small town village on the east coast of England, ' the faggots' and 'pussies' and 'burn in hell' ringing in his ears. 'Not that it matters' wasn't something everyone would say.

"Good to know. I'll see you in third period."

Gareth was to be the first one to ask him about Will. As soon as Alex opened the door to the staff room, there was an on-storm of questions. He was grateful when Abby dragged him away to 'discuss' something with him during lunch break.

"Some of them are like vultures. They did the same to me when I lost the baby. You'd think they'd have some decency, but yeah, no, not really," she said, as she gently nudged him towards the back of the building where students liked to hide and smoke. There were none there at that point, but Alex suspected Abby had made the janitor clear them out so that they could have some privacy on school grounds.

"Well, you prevented me from punching them in the face when, you know, the baby," said Alex.

"More like, I prevented you from getting fired."

"Just saying. I could have helped you back then." Alex shrugged and sat down on the low wall that framed the entrance to the dark 'bunkers' under the school. Abby sat down beside him.

"While we're on the topic of helping-"

"I know." Alex nodded, shoulders slightly stooped.

"No, I'm serious, Alex."

Alex grabbed her hands and pulled her a little bit closer. "Abigail, I know. Thank you."

"Alex?"

"What?" He looked at the worried face that was studying his hands. He tried to pull his jacket over his wrist and knew it was a mistake.

"What happened to your hand?" Her eyes were wide and her brow furrowed and Alex knew exactly where her mind went and hated it.

"Nothing. It's fine." He winced a little when he folded his arms across his chest, pressing the sprained wrist against his chest.

"Alex, those rainbow colours on your skin do not spell 'fine'. Did Will do this?"

Alex rolled his eyes. "Abby? Are you seriously going to pull a 'your partner did this to you'-speech on me?"

She leaned back as if going into defensive position. "No, I'm...but he did, didn't he?"

Alex sighed and got up from the wall. "It was an accident, he was confused after a nightmare. And I'd have hit him right back if I hadn't thought he was about to suffocate just that moment."

Abby looked anything but satisfied. "Abby, accident, I swear. Will is not abusing me with his super special soldier powers. Unless I really want him too." He grinned at her. She smiled back half-heartedly, not entirely convinced yet and absolutely unfazed by Alex's innuendo.

The bell rang across the school grounds. "Come on, I can't be too late or next time they'll think they can just waltz in whenever they like, because 'but Mr Benson, you did that too'," added Alex in a high-pitched voice.

Abby walked a little behind him, sneaking sly glances at his sprained hand. The skin was turning purple and blue, leaving Abby with little doubt as to how much pressure had been on it. She was still staring when Alex suddenly stopped and turned around, causing her to nearly run into him.

"Don't tell Cohen, don't tell Matt, just...don't make a big deal out of it. Please. Will's broken up as it is."

"Broken up *about it*, you mean," said Abby, watching Alex closely.

"Yeah! Broken up about it." Alex quickly turned around, walking towards the entrance to the humanities corridor. He had 13-year-olds waiting for him to tell them all about Napoleon and wasn't that depressing.

13

Will had fallen asleep on the couch, having curled up there after his lunch of leftovers. He'd been trying to concentrate on one of the new books he'd found lying around the house – Alex's purchases from antiquity markets or the small bookshop that already knew the colour of their bedding that's how often they were there. Lara, who had probably sold them hundreds of books already, often talked about arrangements of colours and how some books were too bright to be placed in the bedroom. She was convinced a bright cover would disturb your sleep the same way a bright blue phone screen could affect how quickly you fell asleep. She had helped them work out which colour would best suit their ensuite bathroom when they were deciding for new tiles. More than once, Alex had suggested that she may be in the wrong shop, but then she had always gone into a long speech about all the books that she loves so much, and she would grab the nearest one and start accentuating all the best parts about it. Will was sure Lara had read every book in her shop; her recommendations were usually spot on. The book he had picked up earlier centred around a transgender pianist, something Will would find intriguing on a normal day, but he couldn't keep his eyes moving forward and instead, kept reading the same sentence. He almost felt like he was disappointing Lara and her recommendation. He'd had an image of her sad eyes in his mind before drifting off into an uneasy sleep.

He'd dreamt about the desert again, waking up with an itchy feeling on his face and hands from imagined dust and dirt. His brain was confused by why he was lying down when he should have been standing and on alert, until he heard the doorbell.

"Fuck." He stood up from the couch and didn't think twice about answering the door, twisting the old doorknob left ever so slightly before it properly released and turned right to open. Only when he saw the astounded look on the postman's face did he mentally curse again. The postman gaped, eyes roaming all over Will's left eye and cheek. That morning Will had winced at the sight of himself in the mirror. The film across his pupil seemed to be getting whiter, creating an even starker contrast to the black and blue that still surrounded his eyes. The bruise seemed to have attached itself to Will's face, reluctant to say goodbye and leave behind a lighter canvas. He longed for the day when it would be less noticeable, when perhaps strangers would not stop and stare, but go straight into their spiel of whatever it was that would otherwise grab their attention.

"Yes?" said Will, just wanting the staring to stop.

The postman jerked out of his trance and turned red. "Um..eh..package for Benson," he stammered, now looking anywhere but at Will's face.

Slightly annoyed, Will signed off the package and placed it by the stairs. As he looked up to say goodbye and close the door he noticed the two yellow ribbons tied around the branches of their rhododendron bushes. He stared at them, not sure what to make of them, not sure whether he appreciated the symbolic support. The surprised postman followed his line of vision. Something seemed to dawn on him and he looked at Will and hastily said: "Thank you for your service!"

Will frowned, and decided he didn't like the ribbons. He mumbled a 'goodbye' and quickly closed the door, leaving a very baffled postman out on the steps.

Going into the kitchen, Will tried to tell himself that people were just being nice, that this was the social norm, that this was how it used to be. After he had come home from his first tour, his mum had tied a yellow ribbon around the little lamp that lit up their house number. He remembered letting it flow through his fingers; the soft touch of silk on his rough skin reminding him of how much he'd missed the comforts of home. He had appreciated it back then. This time, however, it simply didn't feel right.

14

Alex got out of his car with a heavy sigh. He was tired. After the night before, 6 classes with students of all sorts of ages with all sorts of problems and a conference about one particularly tough case of 'please pay attention to me, you stupid teachers', he was drained. He had two lessons to prepare for tomorrow; his original plans having become redundant due to heated arguments in one class and extremely quick and detailed work in the other. He should be happy about the progress in the latter, but at the moment, all he could think about was the time the preparations would cost him.

He stopped short at the sight of the yellow ribbons and looked up and down the street as if to see the culprit running away from the scene. He put his bag by the front door and made to untie the ribbons from the bushes. Maybe someone would come by and ask what had happened to them and Alex could explain; or maybe, they'd just be insulted and half the neighbours would stop talking to them. Not that Alex necessarily minded; some people meant too well.

The ribbons were tied rather loosely and Alex made quick work of it, throwing them in the big bins on the side of their house before entering. He hoped Will hadn't seen them. The house was dark and quiet, as if Alex was still on his own and Will was still over in Afghanistan. He walked into the kitchen, saw the kettle on the hob and placed his hand on it to see if it was still warm. The metal was cold, yet the kettle was full, ready to be heated. Alex turned and only then saw the small parcel on the kitchen table.

Sender: *Roger Benson*

Alex cursed under his breath, this was not a good day. Ignoring the parcel for the moment, he went upstairs quietly. For some reason he hoped Will was sleeping. He didn't want to be the one initiating the conversation about the ribbons. The bedroom was dark; curtains drawn and the only light source coming from the hallway.

Will was curled on his side, the blanket wrapped around him tightly like a cocoon. The dark hair was standing on end, as it always did when Will had been asleep for some time. There was always one strand of hair that went up from behind his ear waving at Alex as if to say hello. Alex smiled and closed the door again, going back into the kitchen.

The parcel contained a small souvenir alarm clock of London, a gift card for M&S and a letter written on computer. 'At least he signed it himself,' thought Alex. It was obvious that the 'presents' had been picked by Sally, his father's assistant. It was better than last time, when his father hadn't even so much as acknowledged that Will had returned safely from Afghanistan. At least now he'd sent something resembling a welcome home gift and wished Will good health, presuming his father had actually read the letter before signing it. It was safer to assume Sally wished Will good health.

Alex picked up the phone and dialled Ruth's number.

"Hello, baby brother."

Alex smirked unseen. "Haven't been a baby in quite a while, you know."

"Believe it or not Alex, I have very few pleasures in life. Calling you my baby brother is one of them."

"Pathetic."

Ruth laughed. "Tell me about it. What can I do for you? Do you need a summary of last night's dinner? Suggestions as to what to do with Will's blatantly obvious depression? Or do you want to tell me how Roger didn't call to check on you and Will?"

"Neither. Roger actually sent a parcel with gifts and a letter he signed personally. I mean Sally wrote it, but he actually signed. I'm completely thunderstruck."

Ruth sighed. "I don't want to spoil the nice surprise, Alex, but don't get your hopes up or something."

"Who says I'm getting my hopes up? I'm pretty sure he still hates Will or you know the general idea of me being with a man," said Alex, turning on the hob to heat the kettle. He got out the rainbow teapot Abby had given them on the day they'd moved in together. Cohen had laughed at it and then almost dropped it when Abby had hit him, but Alex liked it, especially since it defied everything that his father had tried to raise him into. It was colourful, unusual and most importantly gay; none of these things were to be found under his father's roof.

"Being more the conventional type this is just Roger following the rules of civilised interaction, if you may. Someone he knows was injured, so he has to at least pretend to pay his respect. You know how he is."

The kettle started to whistle and Alex rushed to take it off the heat, filling the teapot before putting two bags of green tea into the hot water. "He didn't do anything of the sort when Will broke his ribs during that football match with Cohen."

"This is different. He got injured while on duty in Afghanistan. Some people will know this, especially the people in his office. This is more for his benefit than yours because he has to show people he cares and supports the troops and so on." Ruth paused. "Tell me if I'm making you mad at him. I mean, maybe you want to enjoy the attention he's finally giving you and Will."

"Nah, it's good that you're pulling me back to reality." Alex dropped in the chair nearest the door, fiddling with his cup and waiting for the tea to be ready.

"Alex?"

"Yes?"

"I'm going to let you and Will be for a week, but if, by next Sunday, you still sound like that over the phone and look like that when we're sitting together, supposedly having fun, as you did last night, I'm bloody well interfering. I'm not going to let you eat each other up over this."

"Unless it's the good kind of eating each other up?" asked Alex with a slight grin.

"Thanks, I needed that image in my head." Ruth laughed quietly, the sound filling Alex with a warmth that had been missing for the last few days.

"I just need to make him talk to me."

"Good boy. You do that. I have to go, this woman's gotta work till six to earn her living." They hung up, having stopped with sentimental goodbyes when they were six.

"Just have to get him to talk," whispered Alex to himself.

15

The yellow ribbons had gone unmentioned, though Alex once caught him looking out of the window at the bushes with such intensity he was sure Will was looking for a sign of them. Even though Alex got home from work at irregular times throughout the week, Will was always in their bedroom sleeping, or pretending to be asleep – Alex was not sure anymore. He received 'thanks' or 'okay' every now and then, and whenever he tried to lure Will into the living room to simply watch some TV together, Will shook his head, and went back upstairs. As far as Alex could tell, Will wasn't eating much, or at least not with him.

He was becoming more familiar with the different variations of Will's coughs than with his voice. Their friends didn't fail to notice, especially Abby who, as a very good listener, was always on top of the going-ons in school, and the fact that Alex bombarded all his classes with text work and written assignments was a popular topic among the students on Thursday and Friday. Alex was normally a teacher known for his creative approaches to history, conducting stagings of WW1 battles, using flashy PowerPoints that reminded them of the Horrible Histories series or getting students to recreate the social workings of medieval villages in whatever new way he could think of. He was loved for it. Dry text work and unscheduled assignments were the sign of a busy teacher who hadn't had the time to prepare his usual lessons, and Alex knew that his lessons were a conversation point. He could tell that Abby tried to get him to talk to her during Friday lunch break again, but some students started a fight and Alex had to interfere, secretly glad about the disturbance and admittedly a bit too light on the punishment. He managed to sneak out of the school building fast enough to not run into Abby again.

However, instead he was stuck with a talkative Cohen who wanted to be entertained while he waited for Will to wake up. He'd shown up at around five o'clock, by which time Will was still in bed and Alex was of course not inclined to tell Cohen that he was actually only pretending to be asleep. So Cohen waited – and talked, filling Alex in on everything that had been going on in his life, forgetting the fact that it was Will who had been gone for three months and not him. Alex cooked dinner for three people, while at the same time not getting his hopes up that there'd be three people eating it at the same time. After four hours, Cohen finally gave up when Alex told him once more that all the coughing exhausted Will. They hung by the door, when Cohen's face changed from its normal mildly-amused and mischievous expression to one of concern and he opened his mouth as if to say something. Alex waited impatiently, hoping it wouldn't be some impractical piece of advice, hoping that Cohen of all people wouldn't go there. In the end, he didn't, and instead, he hugged Alex.

"I'll be in London for the week, but let's go out together next weekend. Do some hip-jiggling you know." Cohen closed the front door himself, Alex still slightly dumb-founded by the unusual hug to do it himself. He simply stared at the loose bronze knob as it shook from the impact of wood on wood.

He went into the living room with a heavy heart, clearing away the two beer glasses. Once in the kitchen, seeing the leftovers from dinner standing on the hob he had to fight the urge to throw the beer bottles through the windows. He kicked the counter hard, the pain shooting through his foot like a small wake-up call to his anger rather than a pacifier. He leaned on the counter, breathing heavily, fingers clenching on the wood. He remembered the odd 'ignoring phase' when they had some of their more intense fights and he also remembered that these phases had only existed because neither of them had wanted to talk about the issue yet. Having been mostly mutual though, it had always been rather easy to wait for the other to get ready; it was possible to say 'oh well in a few hours, tomorrow at the latest, we'll talk about it and settle things'.

He wanted to say 'I understand', but he wasn't sure he could. It hurt to think that Will didn't want to talk to him, maybe even thought it impossible to talk to him. He looked up, seeing his tired face reflected in the dark window. Maybe it was the glass contorting his features but he thought he looked old, dark shadows under his eyes, sagging skin hanging from his cheekbones. Out of nowhere, it hit him again:

"Alex?"

"Eleanor! Did you get home alright?"

"Alex. He was injured. I don't know how bad, they didn't say."

In his mind, he had gone back to a conversation they had had just before Will had flown out to Afghanistan for the first time. The preparation for this had been different to his tour in Kosovo. It had felt more serious from the beginning and so, it had seemed, Will had taken it more seriously too. Two days before flying out, he had given Alex a piece of paper and simply asked him to read it. Alex remembered how Will had gone out into the garden, looking at the rose bushes, standing on the spot that would give him a view of the river. The letter had contained the four codes.

P1- immediate care needed
P2- intermediate or urgent care needed
P3- delayed care
P4- code black

There hadn't been a need to further explain P4 - Alex simply hoped he would never hear that. But, he remembered that he had needed more information on the others.

"What was the code?" he asked as he ran upstairs to find that letter in his bedside table drawer. He didn't really need it, but felt more comfort in knowing that he could refer to his notes on it.

"What?"

"Which code did they use? Did they say? P1 or P2, P3?"

"P2 they said. P2."

The words 'urgent care needed' glared at him and as much as he heard Will's voice in his head saying that a P2 or P3 were barely anything, he did not quite believe it.

He'd looked at his reflection in the window then too; eyes wide, pale face, hands shaking and mind racing and hoping.

His reflection looked worse now than that day; as if he was about to be sick. He turned away from the window, his eyes roaming across the living room. He missed finding Will there, lounging on the couch, reading a book or playing on his laptop with his feet up on the cushions and waiting for the pot of tea Alex was just making. The couch had never looked less inviting and yet Alex's mind made the decision to spend the night there.

The house was still eerily silent as he went upstairs. He had somehow expected Will to come out of the bedroom once Cohen had gone, but perhaps Will had properly fallen asleep now. It made things easier. He tip-toed across the carpet, making no sound. Will was lying on his side again, facing the window and Alex hesitated.

"Will?" he whispered, but there was no reply. Alex suppressed the anger, grabbed the pillow and his blanket, crumpling them up into a large ball, suddenly not caring whether he was making any noise. Once he was back in the living room, he collapsed onto the couch, still clutching the ball of bedding. He had expected something else. Rummaging for the remote control between the couch cushions, he jammed the power button, the TV springing to life and filling the house with noises. Alex dropped his head on the bedding still in his hands, only half watching the cooking show.

"What are you doing?"

Alex's head snapped up. Will was standing in the door, sweatpants hung low on his hips and wearing a T-shirt that was too big for him. His hair was dishevelled and his right cheek was flushed from the warmth of the bed.

"I'm watching telly," said Alex, knowing how it would infuriate Will, but he wasn't willing to accommodate anymore. Not if he got nothing in return.

Will didn't reply immediately and Alex waited tensely for him to say something, not really seeing what was going on, on the telly.

"Why?"

Alex shrugged. "I fancied it."

Out of the corner of his eye, he fleetingly registered the small but heavy iron elephant statue, a souvenir from Eleanor's trip to Laos, flying across the room. What he couldn't ignore though was the breaking of the screen and the crackling and sizzling sound coming from the TV, as the picture vanished behind cracks and a black hole.

Disbelievingly, Alex dumped the bedding on the couch and flipped around. Will's chest was heaving, his fists clenched and brow furrowed.

"What the fuck, Will?" yelled Alex.

"What are you doing?" Will didn't look in his eyes, instead looked at the couch. Alex gaped at him, a voice at the back of his mind telling him to just deflate and drop it and maybe go out to buy a new TV. He drowned it out.

"Are you serious?"

"I'm-"

Alex cut across him, making Will's anger flare up visibly. "For days you ignore me, you don't talk to me, you spend hours up in the bedroom and don't even react at all when I so much as fucking ask you what you want for dinner. And then the moment I remotely do something similar, you fucking smash the TV? Is this what it's going to be like? You get to ignore me, but I have to be there on your fucking command."

"No, of course not." Will looked like he wanted to run away, rocking on his heels.

"You have not given me any sign that you want me up there with you," Alex pointed his finger towards the ceiling, "and now this. What do you want from me? What do you want me to do?"

Will fidgeted with the T-shirt, pulling it longer than it already was. "I don't want you to sleep on the couch."

"Why not?" Alex knew he was cruel; knew he should be grateful Will had voiced as much as that, but it wasn't enough for him, it didn't solve anything.

Instead of answering though, Will simply walked around the couch and made a grab for the bedding. Alex reacted quickly and leaned down on it, face close up to Will's, closer than they'd been for a week.

"No, Will," Alex choked slightly, but trying to hold the gaze. "Not the way it is right now."

Will slowly stood back up straight again, looking at his boyfriend, expression unreadable. It was a few tense seconds before Will turned on his heels and left the house. Alex flinched as the front door fell shut loudly.

"Fuck!" Alex buried his head in his hands, only just realising that Will had been wearing the T-shirt Alex usually used for the gym.

16

The mid-January air wasn't kind, biting and nipping at every bit of unprotected skin. Will didn't feel it, he simply walked on, down the street and past the brewery. The street lamps were slowly coming to life, a circle of orange light every ten feet. He rounded the corner, following the small path leading to the river. Joggers and skaters were passing him, some doing a double-take trying to get another glance. He turned his face away from the lights into the growing darkness. Reaching the river, he sat down at the edge of the embankment. Staring into the dark depths of the slow-flowing water, he tried to ignore the tingling sensation of being watched by almost every passer-by. The anger had ebbed away the moment he'd slammed that door shut, what was left was...loneliness. And shame. He drew up his knees and laid his head on them, hiding from the world while it grew darker around him. The water was rushing along in front of him, a calming sound as if it wanted to say 'It's okay, everything will be fine'. He felt his throat close up a little, a small lump of pain forming near his Adam's apple. It wasn't a particularly good idea to get sick now, but he didn't want to go back yet to an empty bed and a boyfriend who'd put a painful mirror in front of him. A boyfriend who would be sleeping on the couch tonight for good measure.

A heavy jacket was draped across his shoulders, shutting out the cold almost instantly. Will raised his head, expecting Alex to stand over him, instead, Cohen nodded at him straightening his sweat-shirt before sitting down on Will's left side, forcing him to properly turn his head to be able to see his best friend.

"What are you still doing here?" he asked instead of thanking him.

"Seeing Alex's face, as he closed the door on me, after you kept me waiting for several hours I might add, I figured I should stick around in case you guys needed an intervention or something. So I went down to the pub," said Cohen.

Will looked at the dark water, drawing the jacket closer around his shoulders. "Any excuse to go to the pub," he said with something that resembled a smirk.

Cohen gave him a small smile. "You just don't appreciate the very good pub just down the street, mate. On the other hand, it might not be a good idea for you to start drinking now."

Will jerked his head around, furrowing his brow. Cohen was looking ahead, as if he hadn't said anything at all.

"Could you sit on my other side?" asked Will.

"So you can pretend you're looking at me out of the corner of your eye when in fact you're not. No thanks, make a fucking effort, Will." To make a point, Cohen stretched out his legs, his feet hanging over the edge of the riverbank.

The anger was back and Will threw the jacket off his shoulders and got up, walking further down the river and further away from his home. He heard how Cohen scrambled up and hurried after him, but he didn't slow down.

"You know, Will, you should decide what you want. You want to be treated normally? Don't insist on people accommodating to you," yelled Cohen after him. Several people, on their way home, turned their heads at them. "You want to be alone? Then fucking move out, 'cause what you're doing right now isn't helping either you or Alex. You want to be rid of him? Fucking end it then." Cohen's voice grew angrier with the lack of reaction, but at his last words Will stopped and turned around.

"Who said I want to end it?" There was a mixture of anger, fear and shock on Will's face that made Cohen feel hopeful.

Cohen sighed and rolled his eyes as if things couldn't have been more obvious. "You did, you idiot. Every day of the past week. What do you expect him to think when you don't even talk to him and hide away in the bedroom?"

"He told you that?" shot Will back at Cohen, his voice stumbling over the words in his frustration.

"I just spent four hours with the guy while waiting for you to get your arse downstairs. He didn't have to," said Cohen, his voice calmer now.

Will's eyes darted from Cohen's face into the darkness and back again. "I don't want to end it. There's nothing wrong with us."

Cohen looked at him dumb-founded. "Yes, I'm sure you were out here without a jacket and a brooding expression because there is absolutely nothing wrong with you guys. Normal behaviour of a happy couple, I absolutely agree."

"You know what Cohen, you don't get it and it's none of your fucking business." With these words, Will turned around and walked away.

"Yeah, I don't get it, but neither does Alex," yelled Cohen, watching the receding figure. Too late, he remembered that the jacket was still in his hands. Will, who needed it, long gone.

17

He shivered from the beads of sweat rolling down the skin on his back. It was a strange sensation as his face was burning up at the same time, mercilessly tortured by the sun. The metal of the Ocelot only intensified the scorching rays of light. They were inside a saucepan that was boiling them like fresh lobster. Every other minute, a small droplet of sweat would roll into his eyes, stinging and blinding him. He always blinked repeatedly as if that truly made it better - it didn't; but it was the only thing he could do. His left hand was holding the shaft of his weapon, his right hand was tightly wound around the trigger.

The roads were uneven and more than once, Will banged his helmet against the side of the Ocelot, the noise ringing in his ear. Their platoon was heading towards a small village, for reconnaissance, even though they were not supposed to do reconnaissance, but that never quite mattered with the army. They had been in the area, it was their job now. The other two platoons of their company were a few miles south and west of them. They were meant to meet up at 2400 hours.

Andrew slowed down, the inhabitants of the village now in view.

"The women are running inside, watch your three."

"Running?" It was that more than anything that made Will nervous. People were usually not too bothered, going about their business as usual. Some may have been hiding behind half-open doors or standing just in the corner of the window, but they never had anything to hide. In most villages and small towns, their platoon had been greeted with a nervous curiosity more than anything else. It didn't seem to be a good sign that these women were running into their buildings. Will gripped his weapon tighter, and felt a knot in the pit of his stomach.

"Shit, I don't like this." Jack was shuffling in the back of the Ocelot. Will found he agreed. They were three people in a poorly armoured car and were on point for their platoon. Both he and Jack had to cover more ground than they normally would with four people or even five. Jack was on nine and twelve o'clock and Will on three and six. With Andrew driving and Jack looking out over the desert, it was up to Will to spot anything unusual in that village. He felt a tingling on his neck that had nothing to do with the sweat rolling down.

"I really don't like this. Guys, all I can see is dirt, talk me through. What's on six?" Jack sounded nervous.

"Well, at the moment, a village that looks really fucking empty. Where did they all go? Okay, Andrew drive by slowly."

"Don't you want to stop and get out? You know, do the whole reconnaissance thing?" asked Andrew.

"I think we already fucked that up. They know we're here; not much reconnaissance left to do is there? We probably should have stopped a mile away. But what do you know."

Andrew laughed, it was one of their phrases. "Well, what you don't know, you've learned for next time," he said, imitating their captain's raspy voice. "Unless you're dead."

"Oh come on, don't do that to me." It was Jack's first time out here and it was moments like these that made Will wonder whether he wasn't quite right in the head anymore; when talk about being dead didn't bother him at all.

They were now closing in on the main road - well, pathway. Will wouldn't really call it a road, it was the same sand as everywhere around them, with few signs of people walking on it, let alone cars driving over it. It snaked its way between six houses, with another three off to the left of the centre. Will could make out a well and a few small, wooden sheds close by. He thought he heard the sound of goats coming from them.

"Livestock, not visible."

"Yeah, I heard them too. Jack, your nine?" Andrew was scanning the horizon ahead, concentrated on finding as smooth a path as possible.

"All clear and sandy."

"Fuck!" Will adjusted his weapon, blinked again and edged forward in his seat.

"What?"

"Jack, watch your fucking nine!" yelled Andrew. "Whatever Will does or says is none of your fucking business."

"It is my business if we're about to be blown up."

"And it is even more your business if Will's side is an attempt at distraction and we're about to be blown up from nine o'clock by some douchebags you didn't see because you were too busy looking at someone else's area. So fuck off and watch your fucking nine."

"Shut up, both of you." Will looked through his monocular to get a clearer view. "Three o'clock. I think he's carrying an RPG, walking slowly towards us."

"How sure is your 'I think'?" Even though there was about a foot between them, Will could feel Andrew tensing up. Out of the corner of his eye he saw him grab the radio, ready to call it in.

"Damn, I don't know. It's hard to see, wait. It looks like it. It's a long tin. That's all I can see."

"If you ask me, it's more than suspicious. Alpha 2, receiving."

"Receiving, Alpha 1."

"Please confirm, suspect in possession of RPG, three o'clock."

"Negative, can't be certain, over."

"I'd say 80% sure it's RPG. Wait, he's putting it on the ground."

"Shoot."

And that was all Will needed. 80% and 'shoot'.

18

Rays of early morning sunlight snuck their way through the heavy curtains and into the living room, illuminating the dust that was swirling in the air. Alex could hear the garbage lorry make its way down the street and groaned inwardly at having forgotten to put out the bins. He blinked a few times to scare the sleep out of his eyes and turned his face away from the back of the couch. Will was sprawled in the armchair with his head lolling to the side. His face was slightly screwed up as if in pain and he shivered, despite the thick blanket covering him from neck to toe. Alex sat up, looking closely at Will. Sweat glistened on his brow and the hair at the back of his neck was tickling the skin in wet curls.

"Will?" Alex threw back the thick blanket, chilly air engulfing his body and he went to turn up the heating. One look at the white grass outside told him that the night had been very cold. Will moaned in his sleep and pulled the blanket higher, balling it up underneath his chin. He was still shivering and Alex swore inwardly. He put a hand on Will's forehead – he was burning up.

"Alex?" mumbled Will, stirring slightly. He opened his eyes a small fraction and tried to sit up.

"No! Stay," said Alex, gently pushing him back into the armchair. "How long have you been out in the cold?"

"Don' know." At that moment, Will began to cough violently, the blanket falling from his body and crumbling to the floor. He gripped the armrest as his body jerked forward.

Alex ran into the kitchen, pulled open the top drawer and grabbed the inhaler that he'd placed between the spoons on Monday evening. Forcing it into Will's hand, he held him upright as he drew breath.

"We're going to the hospital," said Alex in a tone that didn't leave room for discussion. He gripped Will's arm tight and pulled him out of the armchair.

"Alex-"

"No, your lungs are coming out of your mouth and you were outside all night with only that ridiculous T-shirt of mine to shield you from the January cold. Seriously, what were you thinking?" asked Alex, pushing Will towards the hallway.

"I wanted to get away," said Will, not looking Alex in the eyes. He grabbed the banister to stay upright as another round of coughs rolled over him. "First from you, then from Cohen."

"Yeah, well Cohen came back and told me about your encounter. And then he yelled at me because I told him he shouldn't have yelled at you," said Alex, smirking.

"What did he say to that?" asked Will, as he unsteadily slipped into his worn-out sneaker.

"That we suited each other and that he was pleased that we were at least equally doomed for stubborn misery." Alex forced Will into a sweat-shirt, followed by a winter jacket. He grabbed one of his longer scarves and tied it around Will's neck. However, as he tried to put a wool hat on Will's head, he received a glare that he'd only seen once or twice since they had first met and immediately threw the hat on the dresser again. Will instead reached for the sunglasses.

"But your hair is wet."

"Unless you're making me go by bus to the hospital, which I doubt, I don't really need it. It's two metres from the door to the car and I'm sick already." Will held out the car key to Alex, who grabbed it with a mixture of a scowl and a grin.

"At least, you're bitchy again," he muttered.

"I'm not bitchy, I'm cynical," answered Will, before opening the front door. The cold air hit their faces, making Alex shiver, though not as much as Will. He was disturbed by more coughs before he made it into the car and Alex checked the glove compartment for the spare inhaler before driving away.

19

It was a feat stopping Eleanor from coming over to Shrewsbury. Alex argued with her for half an hour before she admitted that her being there wouldn't do anything but put Will under more stress. She had the decency to not ask how things were but Alex suspected that she could guess the general situation between them. She let him go on the promise to call at least once a day and whenever anything changed.

Ruth was less willing to stay where she was, charging into the small waiting area like a tornado on wheels. All around the waiting room, heads whipped up, stunned eyes looked around to find the source of the clack-clack of high heels and the jingles of keys and coins in a bag. Ruth was entirely unimpressed by the stares and made a beeline for Alex, who was sitting in the far corner, opposite the toilets. Ruth glided into the seat next to him, crossing her legs in one smooth motion, her arms resting on her knees. Her bag landed on the floor in a less elegant fashion, clanging around the dull room. "How is he? And please explain to me why you let him leave the house with only a T-shirt on?"

Alex rolled his eyes. "Do you guys have like a secret network going on where you tell each other everything that's going on between Will and me?" he asked.

"Of course we do," she said.

Alex knew he should have never given her Cohen's number, or the other way around. "They say he'll probably be in for a few days. They suspect hypothermia, and I heard something of pneumonia. Then they kicked me out. I think, they're doing some tests at the moment, mostly on his lungs."

Ruth nodded and sat back.

"Don't you have to work?"

"They can do without me," she said, waving his comment off.

Alex raised his eyebrows. "Ruth! You'll lose your job again."

She shrugged. "Don't like it anyway. Besides it's like a big summer hole right now, only in winter. They barely have any customers at the moment, some days I get paid for doing nothing, literally."

"Our father won't be too happy if you lose your job," Alex said.

She looked at him sardonically. "If that emotional state of unhappiness were any different from his usual emotional state of unhappiness, I might actually give a shit."

Alex smirked.

"So," Ruth threw her hair back, "do you want me to find out more?"

Alex leaned back, looking at his sister gratefully. "Go ahead." She tapped his knee lightly and went looking for a doctor or nurse to harass. Alex was five when his mother died and remembered very little both about her and the time she spent in the hospital. Ruth had been eleven then and much more aware of everything going on around her. Not that she talked about it. It wasn't until a sombre night nearly seven years on that it came tumbling out of her. It was the day Ruth had received her A-Level results and was what she said appropriately intoxicated. It was the first time she talked about everything. About how they had visited their mother once a week, how their dad hadn't allowed for more, how suddenly, the visits stopped, and how three weeks later, their father had simply told them. Alex remembered being forced into a too warm black suit and a tie that choked him ever so slightly and standing in front of a hole in the ground that meant nothing to him. He remembered how he kept glancing at his mother's picture that had been propped up next to the hole. At the age of five, he couldn't quite make the connection and nobody else bothered to explain it to him. It was Ruth who did, who took care of him, Ruth who always had the information. He smiled to himself ever so slightly. Every time Alex went near a hospital, he didn't think of his dying mum, he thought about Ruth and how she always knew everything and made things better. Always the strong one, the one who coped. Until that night of her A-Level results when she cried and whispered into his ear how she had often wished it had been their father who had died. And even at the age of nearly twelve, he thought he knew exactly what she meant.

A look of success on her face, Ruth came back 20 minutes later with information about Will's room and they went to look for it. They took the lift to the fourth floor where it pinged open onto a corridor that had seen better days. The lower half of the walls was painted in an orange colour that seemed like the faded memory of an unspectacular sunset. In places, the paint was peeling off, leaving dark shadows. The signs directing patrons were greying and peeling on the edges and there were old trolleys lined up along the walls which carried equipment. They easily found Will's room number and quietly opened the door. It led into a dark, small hallway before the room opened up wider, providing the space for two beds. Alex only glanced into the small bathroom right next to the door before checking whether Will was in one of the beds. One bed was empty, sheets perfectly tucked under the mattress.

There was another patient lying in the second bed, sleeping with his back to the window. Ruth pulled the curtain around his bed to give him more privacy before she settled at the small table in the room with Alex. She nodded at the sleeping man. "They told me he's a soldier too."

"You'd think they'd get single rooms and special treatment or something," said Alex.

"But having a fellow soldier with him might be good for Will." Ruth rummaged in her bag until she found her lipstick. "And now tell me, do I need to intervene?" Alex waited for her to pull up her hair in a long ponytail, before he answered.

"I don't think so. I slept on the couch last night."

Ruth raised her eyebrows. She looked fierce with her lipstick, ponytail and crossed arms. "And how is that not a reason for intervention."

"Because I think it helped. You should have been there this morning. He slept in the living-room, in the armchair. He didn't want me to sleep on the couch and he was really angry about it. And this morning, he was almost normal again."

"You make it sound like he was a different species for a week," said Ruth.

"I didn't see the Will I know," replied Alex. "Ruth, he destroyed the TV, like he threw the elephant statue at it on purpose."

Ruth's eyes widened. "Okay, now I'm confused. Do you want me to intervene or not?"

"Can you do a mild version of this intervention?" asked Alex after a few seconds.

"Alex, you're challenging me, but I'm willing to try." She sighed and reached up with her arms.

"Leave the ponytail," said Alex quickly. "Can't hurt."

The man in the other bed stirred. Slowly the curtain was pulled back a few centimetres and Ruth and Alex looked on as he blinked away the sleep in his eyes. Dark locks fell over his eyes, some of them standing on end. He seemed especially pale in contrast to his hair.

"Hi, we're here for Corporal Will Collins. Sorry to have bothered you," said Ruth.

"No, it's fine," croaked the soldier, looking from one to the other, before turning on his side again. The curtain fluttered slightly and left a small gap through which the dark locks were still visible.

He reminded Alex of Will, always turning away, shutting everything and everyone out. Alex had never before thought about how much symbolic power the back of a human can have, it made him feel insecure, like he was intruding on something he had no right to. It was fine with this stranger, but he realised that it frustrated him, when Will, his partner, did it.

As he left his thoughts he noticed Ruth staring at him as if she knew something.

"It'll be good for Will to not be alone in here," she said. "I'm almost hoping he will have to stay for a bit."

"Yeah, maybe," said Alex.

There was a knock on the door, followed by a creak as a doctor entered the room, followed by a throng of what seemed to be medical students. Two of them were in uniform, probably training to be medics out in the field and the doctor beckoned them towards the front. Alex stood up, eager for more information.

"Ms. Collins?" said the doctor, directly looking at Ruth.

"Um, no. Benson. You'll be wanting to speak to my brother Alex here, who is Will's partner," said Ruth, smiling politely. The doctor looked taken aback and glanced down at his notes before coughing uncomfortably.

"Your partner was very lucky. We assume he was in a hypothermic state at some point during that night. As it is at the moment, we would really like to keep him here for a few days to rule out pneumonia. His lungs have suffered from the cold and the oncoming flu, considering they haven't had time to improve much in the first place. This is more than unfortunate. That this happened is quite irresponsible and I must emphasise that you cannot let this happen again. As I understand it, he spent the night outside?"

Ruth's arms had drawn tighter at the warning the doctor gave to Alex, as if Alex had tied Will to the nearest tree and left him there. Before Alex could say anything, she replied: "Yes, that's true. But it's not like we planned on this happening. What do you suggest we should have done to prevent a grown man from making the decision to go outside?"

The doctor paused for a few seconds. "If someone had searched for him and found him early on, any possible damage could have been prevented," said the doctor without looking at Ruth.

Ruth huffed, a sharp breath escaping her nose. Alex knew it wasn't so much what the doctor had said, it was the fact that he hadn't looked at her. It was perhaps her biggest pet peeve: people hiding behind sly looks, hidden faces or worse computer screens. She shook her head, more to herself than anything else. "This implies that you think we didn't," she said.

The doctor ignored her comment, even though a few of the students gave each other meaningful looks. "I have ordered a psychological evaluation for your partner which will take place tomorrow here in the hospital."

"No," intervened Alex, stepping in front of Ruth now.

"Sir, considering the incident –"

"No. Not here. Forget it. Believe me when I say, my partner will check himself out before you've even finished saying 'psychological evaluation'. And I'm pretty sure that that's not what you want, is it?"

The doctor looked as if he would really like to role his eyes. "Sir, I am fully aware that this is a delicate situation that needs careful treatment-"

"I'm sorry, but you're not," said Ruth. "Have you been in the army? Have you actually been to Afghanistan?" The soldier with the dark locks turned in his bed, watching the scene unfolding in front of him.

"Your brother needs psychological treatment that much is clear. He spent the night outside in the middle of January wearing nothing but a T-shirt and with lungs like his he must have known what kind of lasting damage that could do," said the doctor, dropping all efforts at euphemistic explanations.

Ruth raised her eyebrows. "And I understand what you're trying to do and that you mean well, but put yourself in his shoes: You have just gotten injured in Afghanistan, your lungs are permanently damaged, and you're half blind. Wouldn't you think that a person who then runs out into the cold January night because he was upset needs someone other than an unqualified hospital psychologist? Yes, unqualified," said Ruth, as the doctor was just about to interrupt her, "unless you can tell me that the psychologist you want to send Will to is an expert in post traumatic stress disorder due to warfare experience?"

"No, he isn't." They all turned towards the dark-haired soldier. He was sitting now and they could see the bandages on his left arm and up his shoulder. He looked even younger now, in his loose hospital gown and his feet barely reaching the floor. "I don't think any of them are."

Ruth smiled at him and then watched the doctor's mouth fishing for words and not finding any.

"The only information I now want from you is when my brother's partner will be put in this room so we can see him," said Ruth, breaking the silence.

The doctor looked at the charts in his arm. "They're doing a peak flow test at the moment, but it shouldn't be more than half an hour before he'll be here."

"Thank you." Ruth inclined her head before sitting back down and Alex followed suit. Alex mouthed 'What the hell is a peak flow test?' at Ruth. She shrugged, but just like him didn't ask. Alex didn't really feel like having any further conversation with the doctor at the moment. He could always google it.

The doctor and his medical students turned towards the other soldier who was still sitting up. After a quick but embarrassed-sounding cough, the doctor asked a few questions about the soldier's physical well-being, making notes. He pulled up the bandages with one hand, charts still clutched in the other and talked to his students. "As you can see, we have a case of third-degree burns here. It's healing very slowly and the patient has torn open the scar tissue, resulting in infected blisters settling between the healing scar tissue."

The medical students were allowed to examine the arm and shoulder before the doctor ushered them all out of the room with one last glance at Ruth and Alex. As soon as the door closed, the dark-haired soldier leaned forward even more. "I kind of wish you had been here three days ago."

"You've had the pleasure of meeting the hospital psychologist?" asked Ruth.

"Yeah. I'm Ben." He smiled, somehow making him look younger still. It was impossible to tell how old he actually was, his face saying 20, but his eyes saying 98.

"Ruth and this is Alex, my brother and Will's partner."

Ben's eyes widened. "So you're not married then?" he asked Ruth, not even looking at Alex.

"No I'm not. Free as a bird." said Ruth, without blushing even the slightest bit.

"And just as difficult to handle," said Alex, getting a smack on the arm from Ruth.

"Ruth, stop hitting my boyfriend." Will was sitting in a wheelchair, pushed into the room by a nurse. He looked even more ill dressed in a hospital gown with his pale skin shining against the light and vividly highlighting the sunglasses he was still wearing. The middle-aged nurse parked him right beside his bed and he climbed up. Switching the intravenous injection from the chair to a stand next to the bed, she reminded them that visiting hours were technically over and dinner would soon be served.

As soon as she was gone, Ruth placed herself in front of Will. "So, he's your boyfriend again, is he?"

It was Alex's turn to hit his sister lightly on the arm.

"What? You told me to intervene."

"A mild version I said," reminded Alex.

"That was mild," said Ruth.

"It had cynicism and a direct approach in it, how is that a mild version?" Behind them Ben was laughing quietly.

"Fine, I won't do it then. I'll just hit the loo and then we can go. Will, this is Ben. Make him your new best friend, he seems much more suitable than Cohen." She disappeared to the toilet attached to the room, narrowly missing the plastic cup Will had thrown at her.

There was a short silence. "How are you feeling?" The shivering had stopped and the hair at the back of the neck was dry again, but Will still looked pale and drained.

"My ribs hurt. You asked her to do an intervention?" Will was scrutinising Alex who put his hands into his pockets.

"Yeah, well, you know me." Alex didn't look at him.

Will frowned. "Yeah, exactly. I know you."

Before Alex could reply anything, Ruth returned, kissing Will goodbye. Alex leaned down to give Will a peck on the lips, but it felt awkward for him and their lips touched only momentarily.

"I'll bring your mobile, your netbook and your book tomorrow. Anything else?"

"A few cookies and some juice. I doubt I'll get any in here."

"Okay." Alex hesitated, eager to say more, say something else, but he left it at that. "See you...see you tomorrow." He waved awkwardly, before stuffing his hand in his jeans pocket.

*

"That was weird," said Ruth once they were in the lift to the ground floor.

Alex nodded in agreement. "Never do an intervention for me again."

"I hadn't even started it."

"Never even start an intervention for me again," corrected Alex.

"Got it. Never again."

20

Alex came by early in the morning to check on him and bring some of his clothes. Will's fever had gone up with continuous fits of coughing shaking his body. The doctors and nurses looked worried and shared their pitiful looks with Alex. They didn't talk much and Will knew Alex didn't feel like it in front of a stranger. It was difficult enough when they were on their own. Alex left again with an awkward hug and the promise to return the next day after work. He turned back with a sad smile, just before he turned the doorknob. Will wished he'd have smiled back.

Will didn't fail to notice that Ben didn't get any visitors and suspected that he was eager to talk to someone. To Will, it was somehow strange to be around someone with a similar background and problem again. He'd detested lying in the hospital in Bielefeld, surrounded by depressed soldiers; had avoided talking to these men who lost a leg, an eye or their minds. It just made things worse instead of better, like a three-months long monsoon after two months of draught. You would expect relief and in his case, most people would have expected him to be glad to talk about his experiences, but he didn't share that sentiment.

No, he hadn't talked to anyone. Least of all anyone he knew. Apart from Alex and Cohen and Abby, who he'd avoided talking on the phone to, there was also Captain Leon Fitzgerald – what a name for a Captain – whose experience and strategic thinking were almost infamous. He'd been injured by a rogue grenade that was meant for the enemy. Sometimes, Will thought he was searching out someone to talk to. They'd worked together in Iraq in 2009 and even though Will had been well beneath him rank-wise, Captain Fitzgerald seemed to recognise him. He looked lonely, but Will couldn't bring himself to talk to him and instead, always fled when he saw him approaching. The one time he failed to do so, Captain Fitzgerald kept asking questions about Will's private life that Will didn't even want to begin to think about it. It took him 20 minutes to finally get away from him and hide underneath his blanket, pretending to be asleep, feeling guilty on more than one level.

Now, Will was confined to his bed, more so than in Bielefeld, because of the suspected pneumonia. If he wanted anything, needed anything, he'd have either the nurses, who looked at him strangely, or Ben, who was nice, eager to talk and reminded Will of himself.

Ben was a Lance Corporal, as Will had been two years prior. He'd just been promoted to this rank two days before an RPG bomb ripped his Humvee apart and set half his body on fire. His face was mostly unharmed, except for two small burn scars that almost looked like moles. Will envied him for it. His mother had been a drunk and his father had cared even less about him. He had joined the army because he had thought there wasn't anything else he could do. He still wasn't properly educated and now invalided for life.

"But I don't regret it," he added hastily, trying to shake off the bitter taste after his life story. "It gave me something proper to do. Like, I had a purpose, you know?"

Will nodded. He knew how that felt. That was before, when the job still made sense.

"Why did you join?" asked Ben, looking interested, not judging like so many others who had uttered that question.

Will remembered the fight he'd had with his mother. She'd tried so hard to convince him to go to college, to do something, anything else.

'You like nature, why don't you do something where you can work outdoors. Landscaping or something. They've got some nice colleges for that. You know we have the money.'

He smiled ruefully. Maybe he should have listened to her, instead of going to his dad's grave to solemnly promise that he would join. "My dad, well, and my granddad. Well, I'm not sure they actually meant for me to join, but they kind of always wanted to join. I think both kind of regretted not having done it when they had the chance. My granddad couldn't, but my dad, I think he missed the chance. Instead, he took up a job at a local animal shelter and stayed, and stayed a bit longer. Then he met my mum, and six months later she was pregnant, three months after they were getting married and once I was there, he didn't think he could go. When we went on holidays, granddad and him always took us to some military places. We went to Scotland just to go to the War Museum inside the Edinburgh Castle and to Fort George near Inverness. My dad pretended we were there for the Highlands, the scenery and Loch Ness, but we weren't. He had all sorts of military memorabilia and I don't even know why it interested him. I never asked, maybe it had something to do with my grandfather, maybe my dad was just wired like that."

Will shrugged, turning his head to look out of the window. He'd been one of these men who'd never questioned why they'd joined. He'd simply done it and that was that.

"Maybe my dad never wanted me to sign up," said Will quietly. It wasn't the first time he had that thought.

"What happened? To your father, I mean? If you don't mind me asking," added Ben hastily.

"Really stupid actually. He said so himself. He'd forgotten to freshen up his anti-rabies inoculation. One day, his favourite lizard escapes again, goes into one of the dog cages and my dad has to get him out. Something bites him in the leg, just a nip really, but it isn't a dog, just a small bite and he thinks he has had his inoculation, so he patches it up and goes home. He tells us about a bite, but that's normal at the animal shelter, he's been bitten before. We don't think anything of it, until a month and a half later. He gets this serious infection. Three days later, he is dead. Once it's in the blood or in the brain, there's nothing they can do. It was a rat. It was a rat bite. Got in under the loose floor covering in the corner." Will sighed. "A fucking rat."

"Inside a dog cage. It's ironic, really," said Ben. His eyes widened in horror. "Oh god, I'm sorry, I didn't mean to be disrespectful...I-"

Will laughed. "Look at us being all cynical about death."

"Isn't that part of the job description?"

21

Abby leaned against the door frame, eyes fixed on the spot where the TV used to be. Alex rummaged through the cupboards to get cups and spoons out, furtively glancing at Abby every now and then. Her shoulders were squared and that meant that she was preparing for something big. Once she was in that mode, she managed to get the entire humanities department equipped with whiteboards, or organise the complete funding for two separate school plays.

He'd known something was coming. The moment he told her over the phone that Will was in the hospital he'd known. He was also really starting to wonder how often his sister communicated with his friends. It was disconcerting.

"Are you going to buy a new one?"

Alex shook his head. "Can't afford it." He stirred a spoonful of sugar into Abby's cup. "Well, I suppose I could afford it, but we don't need it and right now, I'm not sure whether we might not need the money for something else at some point."

Abby frowned. "What do you mean? Will was insured, right?"

"Well yeah, for the initial injury and even then, it's only up to like 7,000 pounds in most cases. I've done a bit of research. Anyway, I'm sure they're going to cover deliberate worsening of the state of your health," added Alex sarcastically.

"If not, there's still NHS. And besides, he lost an eye for Christ's sake. I know for a fact that they pay more for that," said Abby, reinforcing her words by poking Alex's arm several times. "I did my research too."

"Yes, you did. The problem is both semantic and physical. He lost *an* eye," said Alex. "He can still see with the other one."

"Shit."

Abby went to the couch and sat down, picking up yet another shard of broken plastic from the TV that Alex had missed during the clean-up. She put it on the table and gestured to the bit of free couch next to her.

Alex sat down with a heavy sigh, in anticipation of the lecture that was to come. Abby started right away.

"Are you angry at him because he broke the TV, because he broke himself more, or because he ignored you for almost two weeks?"

"You have got to stop talking to Ruth. *I've* got to stop talking to Ruth."

"Consider us your support system. There needs to be connection and communication within a support system, otherwise what's the point and now answer my question." She looked at him sternly.

"Well, basically...you know, I'm not really angry at him, per se. I mean yeah, I'm..it pisses me off that he ignores me and at the same time, he expects me to be there for him apparently, and it doesn't make sense and he's behaving like a child and the whole fight we had before he ran out was just pointless," rambled Alex. He threw his head onto the backrest of the couch. Abby's hand flew up to stroke his hair and he closed his eyes.

"And why are you really angry?"

Alex knew the answer, but he wasn't sure whether he really wanted to admit to it. Saying it out loud felt like breaking something that was hanging on the thinnest of threads already anyway.

"I can't read him anymore. I used to be able to read him so well, to know what he was thinking, what he was planning on doing, what he wanted. It's like all of that is gone now. He's still him, but he's also not. It scares me how much he confuses me. It's like my brain can't cope with this new person, because he's not actually new. He's not supposed to be anyway."

Abby's fingers had halted while Alex spoke, but at his final words, they resumed their path through his hair. She had to swallow twice before she dared to ask the next question for fear of choking.

"Do you think you'll get him back?"

It was Alex's turn to swallow the heavy lump in his throat. "I don't know." He remembered the short moment in the hallway when things had been like they used to be; them scrabbling over who was going to get the car for the day or who would have to do what while they danced around each other trying to get ready on time. Most of the time, Alex arrived at school with two scarves in his bag, because Will didn't wear them, but Alex kept on trying to convince Will to wear one until he was kicked out in front of the school. Will never wore a scarf.

"Will never wears a scarf," whispered Alex.

"What?" asked Abby, looking confused.

"He never wears a scarf. We fight about him not wearing scarves because I don't want him to get sick and he doesn't give a shit about that."

"Okay. So?"

Alex sat up straight, leaving Abby's fingers hovering in air where his head had just been. Alex's hair was slightly standing on end, but he was elsewhere, looking at the memory. "So, he let me put a scarf around his neck before we went to the hospital. He glared at me and complained and denied a hat, but he let me put on the scarf."

"And?" asked Abby. Alex could see a smile now playing around her lips, but his excitement disappeared as quickly as it came.

"And I don't know. It's like that moment before we left was normal, but now that I realise that he let me do that I'm sort of thinking again that things aren't normal."

Abby sighed, exasperated. "Alex."

"What?"

"He let you because he knows it means something to you. That's actually the most reassuring thing you've said all day, to be honest."

Alex looked as if he didn't quite believe her. She kissed him on the forehead and got up from the couch. "Anyway, despite that or well, also kind of because of that, all that, I've done some more research and found three psychologists you together or he alone can try out."

"Abby," said Alex. He followed her out into the hallway, where she rummaged in her bag. A pack of tissues fell out and Alex bent down to pick it up. He would have liked to be able to say, that this was unnecessary, or a bad idea or anything, really, but he found himself tongue-tied. Straightening back up, he was facing Abby holding out a small envelope that could have contained a Christmas card. There was nothing written on it, but its eggshell colour seemed blinding.

"He needs it, Alex. He can't do it on his own, if anything, his behaviour since he got back has proven that he can't do it on his own. Neither can you. And time might help with healing, but it's not enough, in fact I think it might just make it worse the longer you wait." Abby pushed the envelope with the addresses and phone numbers into Alex's unwilling hands.

Alex simply shook his head, turning the envelope in his hands. It didn't volunteer any answers. "He won't do it, and I can't force him."

"He has to. Small gestures like letting you put on a scarf are a light at the end of the tunnel, but they're not going to be enough." She sighed heavily. "Now, these are not the military psychologists because I wasn't sure whether Will is still going to be under military contract or not. So, I don't know yet whether these psychologists slash therapists have any experience with soldiers, mind you, living in Shrewsbury I don't see how they can't, but they're supposed to be good, and I was planning on going tomorrow afternoon to just ask them about their experience. I thought you might want to come with me."

Alex walked past her into the kitchen to put the cup in the sink. He laid the envelope into the half-empty fruit bowl, and leant on the counter, arms crossed.

"I'm going to the hospital in the afternoon. Besides, like I said, it's Will's choice."

"And who is the only person that could give him the push in the right direction?" asked Abby.

"And who says it's the right direction?" Alex rounded on her and met her exasperated eyes. "I'm sorry, Abby, I don't know what to do, but right now this doesn't feel right either, especially without asking Will first."

Abby took a step closer, loosely folding her hands in front of her. It was turning into a lecture. "I know that he has to be asked first, I just think that you should give him the push, because he will listen to you. And...he needs someone to talk to."

"He can talk to me," defied Alex.

Abby rolled her eyes. "Yeah, well, and how is that going for you?" Her eyes widened the second that she said it, but Alex felt his fingers tingle and his hands shake. He could feel the slow burn of oncoming tears of frustration and the close-up throat that tried to shut down the anger. "I think you should go."

"I'm sorry." Abby paused and held out a hand in a pacifying gesture, almost touching his ,arm. "He needs someone to sort his thoughts and issues, someone other than you, you're too close to him. It's the one time that that's a bad thing."

"Abby, please go." Withdrawing her hand, she waited a few seconds for him to look at her. She turned slowly and went into the hallway. He could hear the rustle of her coat and the sharp sound of the zips on her boots. She stepped back into the doorway, her hair slightly dishevelled from the scarf and the hood of her winter coat.

A few seconds went by without either of them speaking and then she murmured: "I'll see you at school tomorrow."

The moment the door fell closed behind her, Alex grabbed the envelope from the fruit bowl, crumbled it into a ball and hurtled it towards the living room, as far away from him as he could within the confines of the house. A wall of anger rose up in him and he turned, facing the counter - facing the window - and remembering Friday night, when this whole mess had exploded on him.

"Fuck, fuck, fuck, fuck!" he said, kicking the cupboards with his feet, the dull sound echoing around the kitchen and nearly drowning his curses, but not his frustration.

22

It was dark around him and as usual, his NVG didn't work properly, the dying batteries cracking the image every few seconds. He heard Andy's footsteps behind him, the rustling of the M.O.P.P. suit and the quiet clanking of the rifle in his hands. The dirt underneath his feet was crunching loudly in his ears. The small hamlet up ahead was doused in silence and darkness. The wind was still – for once in weeks – making the night cloudless and bright as a shopping mall.

"Can we take these things off? I'm sure I'd actually see more without the bloody NVG," whispered Will.

"Do what you have to do and shut up," answered Andy.

Will pulled the NVG off and stowed it in its appropriate pocket on his M.O.P.P. suit.

"The lieutenant's going to kill you." Andy was drawing level with him now, eyes on nine o'clock.

Will grinned to himself.

The explosion to their left didn't swipe them off their feet although it should have, but Will's grin was suddenly wiped from his face as a wall of dirt engulfed him. For a few seconds, he couldn't see. His finger tightened around the trigger and he blinked furiously to clean his eyes. He could feel the grains of sand scraping across his left eye.

A shadow moved towards him, coming closer quickly as if it was running. He breathed in, ignoring his eye, the moment he saw who it was, he could shoot. He was ready, all senses perked. The figure ran faster and Will could make out clearer contours. A rifle was hanging on a strap vertically against its leg. He knew he should shoot. He should really shoot. A wind blew past him, lifting the dust; and suddenly he saw himself, running at him, screaming, mouth open wide, eyes wild with anger. He wore no helmet, holding the rifle steady at his side, and he was screaming. He didn't slow down, he gained speed, his other hand curled in a fist. He didn't slow down.

Will pulled the trigger, crumbling to the floor at the same time as his other self.

In his darkness, two hands found him, gripping his neck tightly. His hands shot up, beating against familiar arms, clawing and scratching. Blood dripped on his face. He screwed his eyes up, keeping them shut, pulling and tearing at those hands. His mouth opened, but no air came in.

He tried to lash out, but unlike Alex, Ben knew what he was doing.

"Will! Wake up!" He could feel the sting of Ben's slap across his right cheek and the tight grip on his arms. He sagged into his pillows, the tension draining out of him. His chest felt tight and he badly wanted to be home in his own bed.

"You can let go now," he murmured, his wheezing lungs accompanying him, and Ben released his arms.

"You okay?"

Will leaned forward to his bedside table, grabbed the inhaler and took a deep breath. His lungs opened up immediately, letting in the freshness of oxygen. The unnatural sounds they made grew steadily quieter. Inhaler still in hand, he fell back against the pillow, turning towards the wall and away from Ben.

He took his cue and returned to his own bed. The sheets rustled and the bed frame creaked. Lying on his side restricted Will's lungs to more shallow breathing, but he couldn't bear for Ben to see him, to watch him.

Just as Will thought Ben had drifted off to sleep again, his voice carried across the room. "I have them too. Not so much anymore, you'll have them less and less. And like, the fireball in my dreams is getting smaller and smaller. It'll be a match light soon, prob-"

"Stop." Will curled in on himself, face half-hidden in the pillow.

A minute passed in almost complete silence, only the wheezy sounds of Will's lungs echoed around the sterile, minimally furnished room.

"Just if you need someone to talk to, I'm..I'm here." Ben was almost whispering. He waited some time - waiting for an improbable answer - before also turning to his side and going to sleep.

23

Alex was lucky his students liked him. He could imagine he looked like shit the way they were all on tenterhooks, talking quietly – almost whispering – during group or partner work and not talking at all when he was explaining things. They didn't moan about having to read much more than usual and didn't call him out on his mistakes on the board. Gareth even brought him coffee every morning from Tuesday onwards.

He'd hoped Abby would greet him as usual and pretend that the fight at the weekend hadn't happened, but she didn't. She greeted him, but it was distant and sad. Temperature in the teachers' lounge dropped by 10 degrees, or so it felt. Colleagues asked after Will, and Alex kept them up to date, but that was all the conversation he got involved in.

Meanwhile, visits to the hospital each afternoon didn't do much to improve his mood. Will didn't seem to sleep well, making him even grumpier than usual. Up until Thursday, Alex thought by 'not sleeping well' Will meant he'd only get a few hours of sleep instead of the proposed 7 to 8. However, he was corrected by Ben once Will was out of the room for yet another test.

"He's not really sleeping at all, I think," he said, startling Alex where he sat next to the window watching the birds on the trees outside.

"What do you mean?" asked Alex.

"Since Sunday, he's had a nightmare every night. I think it's the hospital that's making it worse." There was a slightly haunted look about Ben, indicating that Will wasn't the only one disturbed by bad dreams.

"Every night?"

"Yeah. Not sure what they're about, but he looks terrified after. Doesn't remember where he is for a second."

Alex unconsciously touched his wrist. "Every night. He didn't have that at home, or else I slept through it."

Ben shook his head. "Hospitals are terrifying, especially for soldiers, I think. No one wants to be here, least of all us. It means shit went down."

"Does he talk to you?" asked Alex before he could stop himself, not sure whether he really wanted to know the answer.

"Not about his accident, no – if that's what you mean," said Ben.

Alex tried to make his face look like he didn't really care, that he was cool with whatever. "And other things?"

"Um yeah. Like everything, family, Afghanistan, boot camp. I mean, not all the time; he's quiet a lot, but yeah, we talk." Ben shrugged, but his eyes were boring into Alex. "I take it you don't."

Alex huffed a dry laugh and tousled his hair in a gesture that almost looked like desperation.

"He doesn't really know me, I'm new. That makes it easier," said Ben in a comforting, mediating voice. Alex heard the words, but they didn't have the effect that Ben was looking for. Instead, they passed right over him and out of the open window.

There was a knock on the door and Ben called permission to enter. Expecting to see Will, Alex had sat up, but instead, Ruth entered.

"Hello, little brother. Hi Ben. Why the long faces?"

"I don't have a long face," said Alex.

"You're doing an excellent job of it at the moment," said Ruth, kissing the top of Alex's head. Her eyes asked him if he was okay; he nodded imperceptibly.

"Ben, I like you, but what did you do to my brother?" asked Ruth without looking at Ben. He spluttered and stuttered, his eyes flitting towards Alex.

"Leave it Ruth, it's not his fault." Alex brought a hand up to her arm to reassure her. He felt very tired again; tired of the constant worry, tired of the constant battle everybody else seemed to be fighting for him trying to make things better. So far, it had only resulted in big arguments and admittance to the hospital.

Ruth, however, usually knew when it wasn't worth fighting, so she turned and smiled at Ben. "I brought you that DVD we talked about on Wednesday."

"Wednesday?" asked Alex.

"I was here on Wednesday. You know, visiting. You had a long day, I knew you'd come late." There was a pale blush lighting up Ruth's face.

"Just wanted to keep the boys some company, huh?" Alex couldn't hide the smirk. Most men fairly quickly got the stamp 'Idiot' from Ruth. It had been some time since Alex had seen her remotely flustered by male company. Which of course meant he had to make fun of it.

"Ignore him," said Ruth to Ben, leaning down to kiss him on the cheek.

Alex felt a pang of jealousy at how simple and uncomplicated it looked, even though they'd only known each other for six days.

The door opened again and this time, Will was rolled into the room by the nurse. His anything-but-good mood, was clearly reflected on his face. "I can actually walk, especially since they just told me in your close proximity that I'm allowed to go home."

The nurse was just as bad-tempered as her patient. "And I've told you before, it's hospital policy. I would have thought someone like you would abide by the rules," she answered sharply.

"Well, I'm not in the army anymore, so fuck the rules. Can I get out of this damn chair now?" Will glanced at Alex as he said that, and whatever he saw didn't make him happier.

"Yes, you can," said the nurse and Will quickly stood up, coughing once as he straightened himself up, as if his lungs had to get adjusted to the unusual posture. "But only to get dressed, I have to escort you out of the hospital in that chair."

Will turned around. "You're kidding, right?"

"Believe it or not, I'm not really happy about it either at the moment. Do you need help getting dressed?"

"No, I think I can manage, thanks."

The nurse sighed. "Fine, I'll be back in ten minutes to let you out. And you still have to sign the release form." She left, looking helplessly at Alex, as if asking him to do something about Will. The moment the door closed again, however, it was Ruth who stepped up to Will and kissed his half-naked shoulder. He flinched and turned, surprise on his face.

"It's not her fault. She's just doing her job," said Ruth quietly. Will nodded, before focusing on his bag again, dumping his few essentials into it before grabbing jeans and a t-shirt and disappearing in the bathroom.

Alex watched as Ruth simply turned to Ben again, as if nothing special had happened. "It's a good thing I brought you the DVDs today, or else, you'd be really bored now."

"Yeah, thanks." He smiled, but looked somehow subdued at the same time.

The nurse returned just as Will was sitting down in the wheel chair without complaining. She smiled at Alex, looking pleasantly surprised with this new behaviour. Alex held the door open for her as she wheeled Will out of the room.

"Ruth?"

"I'll be right out in a minute," she said, one of her hands on the rails of Ben's bed.

As Alex followed Will, he saw the doctor taking over from the nurse and pushing the chair into a far corner, mouthing a 'just a minute' in Alex's direction. Alex didn't like it, but since the doctor clearly wanted this to be a confidential meeting, he didn't have much of a choice but to step away. Instead, he leaned against the wall and closed his eyes, remembering Will's surprise at that shoulder kiss. If he wasn't too mistaken, there was something like yearning on his face as well.

"Do you think that's a good idea?" He opened his eyes and saw Ruth nodding towards the doctor and Will in the far corner. The doctor was talking animatedly while Will listened with raised eyebrows and a continuously darkening expression.

"It looks like exactly the kind of reaction we told him he'd get from Will if he dared mention psychologists," said Alex, shrugging half-heartedly.

"Yeah, he can handle it himself. He doesn't look like he's going to be persuaded anytime soon."

"How do you do that?" interrupted Alex.

"Do what?"

"Touch him, kiss him on the shoulder like that. We haven't... I haven't – it's like he's always turning away from me or getting out of my reach. So, how do you do that?"

"Maybe you have to surprise him. You know, attack him from behind and smooch the living daylights out of him," said Ruth, a playful smile on her lips.

"Ruth, I'm serious. I just really don't know what to do. I feel so fucking clueless and helpless and I never know how to be around him anymore and it's driving me mad. He's talking to Ben about stuff, but not to me." Alex rubbed his eyes with the palms of his hands before ruffling up his hair even more, strands of it standing on end now.

"It takes time," said Ruth calmly, but it made Alex even angrier.

"Stop saying that, why does everybody say that? What do I fucking do in the meantime so that when *that* time comes, he's not already gone? Ruth, I mean it, he's literally not fucking talking to me."

Ruth stepped closer, placing one hand on his chest to calm him. "I don't really have an answer either. Just be there, reach out, make sure that – show him that you're there for him and then...then he will probably open up." She knew it wasn't much reassurance, but she had nothing else to give. She looked over his shoulder, sighed and stepped back, taking her hand away. "They're done talking."

As he passed, the doctor nodded glumly at them, before waving a nurse over to push Will's wheelchair. Will was waiting in the corner, a frown on his face as he stared at the two Bensons. The same nurse as before started rolling Will towards the lift, seemingly in a hurry to get him out of there. Alex and Ruth slipped into the lift just as the doors were closing.

As soon as they reached the glass entrance, the nurse stopped the wheelchair abruptly. "You may walk now."

Will put on his sunglasses and got out of the chair. "Thank you. Have a nice weekend."

Ruth left them at the car park, saying she still needed to get some work done. She made to kiss Will on the cheek, but thought better of it half-way there and simply squeezed his shoulder. She did the same with Alex, and he knew she was consciously trying to treat them equally. They watched as her green Skoda drove out of the car park.

Will started coughing once they sat in the car and Alex almost suggested taking him back inside the hospital, but one draw from the inhaler settled the upset lungs. They drove along silently, the ride from hospital back home taking about 20 minutes. At a red light, Will suddenly turned his head and stared at Alex, as if he was looking for something.

"You okay?" he asked.

Alex took his eyes from the traffic light. For a moment, he thought about telling the truth, but at the same time, he just wanted to get home. The car was not the right time. "Yeah, I'm fine."

The light switched to green, a car honked behind them and Alex was more confused than ever. He wondered whether he should say more. Two streets on, Will broke the silence.

"We've got to stop lying to each other."

Alex looked at the street straight ahead, mainly because he didn't know how to reply to that. The atmosphere in the car was suffocating and he was glad when he could park the car in front of their house ten minutes later. They got out simultaneously, but Alex walking up the path first as he had the key.

The silence spread between them as they untied their shoes and hung up their jackets. The house seemed cold all around them, as they stood in the hallway. Will's eyes flitted towards the living room and the corner where the TV stood, he didn't say anything though. He pointed towards the small bag with his essentials.

"Well, I'm going to-"

"You heard what Ruth and I said at the hospital, didn't you?" asked Alex, drowning the thoughts that he shouldn't be doing this now.

Will shook his head. "Not really, you just looked angry and frustrated." His voice lacked emotion; it was like he was holding back on something.

"More like helpless," said Alex, before he could stop himself, hoping that it would have an effect on Will. His eyes widened, the sparse sunlight in the hallway reflected in them.

"But not hopeless, right?"

"No." Alex paused, wondering whether he should hug Will. He decided against it. "I'm going to make dinner. Just come to the kitchen with me, you don't have to talk, you can read a book or magazine or whatever, just don't barricade yourself in the bedroom. Please."

For a moment, Will looked as if that was exactly what he had planned on doing, but he nodded nonetheless. "I'll just bring this up." He grabbed the bag and slowly walked upstairs. Alex watched him, begging anyone who'd listen to make Will come back down again.

By the time the potatoes were peeled, Will returned. He sat down at the dinner table, opening a brand new book from their 'pile of random'. They were those books that jumped out at them in a second hand bookshop; the kind of books that looked interesting but weren't reading priority or recommendations. They were the kind of books that could be hit and miss. There had been some quite awful ones that only looked pretty on a bookshelf, which is where they were, never to be read again. But there had also been some very good ones, some of Alex's favourites, randomly picked up, read months later and loved ever since. As Will sat down with a short book that showed a cat on the cover, Alex thanked whoever had listened and started to prepare the stuffed courgettes. The rustling of the pages and the clunk of the tea cup on the table were the soundtrack to his cooking and for once, it felt like home again. If Will's quiet laughter was anything to go by, the book with the cat on the cover seemed to be one of the better random ones. Alex made a mental note to snatch it from Will later for a quick read.

24

He woke up with a muffled cry, his heart missing two beats and his throat feeling tight again. He fumbled for the inhaler, almost knocking over the alarm clock.

"Will?" whispered Alex sleepily.

Will pushed the top of the inhaler, the sharp sound of medicated air echoing in the dark room. "It's fine, Alex. Go back to sleep."

The sheets rustled loudly and then the small bedside lamp came on, Will seeing the end tails of the light reflected in the window. A small light like this put his half-blindness into a strange perspective. His peripheral vision always included his own nose now; and in this low light, his vision seemed almost two-dimensional.

"Are you sure? You're all wet," said Alex, feeling the pillow cover on Will's side. Alex was right; Will was sweating profusely, like he'd just run twenty miles with the full 10 kilo equipment on his back. "You have to change your clothes. Come on."

The sheets rustled again and Alex's side of the bed rose slightly, as the weight left it. Will heard the creak of the cupboard doors, one of them coming into his line of vision along with one of Alex's arms. He was rummaging through the old and ugly t-shirts as well as the boxers. Will just sat there, and wished Alex away; and then felt horrible for wishing that.

The doors creaked close and Alex came to his side of the bed, placing the T-shirt and boxers next to him. "You have to take off your old clothes first, you know? That's usually how it works," he teased.

Will moved slowly; he just wanted to go back to sleep without Alex saying anything, he wanted Alex to turn around and leave him alone.

A hand brushed along his left cheek and he knew Alex was wiping away tears he couldn't control coming from his injured eye. "Will," he whispered.

"I'm fine," he answered hoarsely, angrily swiping Alex's hand away. Alex stepped back and watched him change the T-shirt; he watched him change the boxers and it felt awkward, worse than the first time they'd both seen each other naked. Then he turned around to start pulling the sheets off and it woke Alex out of his stupor, who reached out for the duvet and opened the zipper at the end.

"Why are you crying?" asked Alex, carefully emphasising the question, so as not to suggest he was accusing Will.

"It's nothing," said Will, throwing the sheets on the floor without looking at Alex. He could feel his stare though, a tingle settling in the back of his neck. He grabbed the pillow, while Alex dumped the naked duvet on the bed.

"Do you really think I care? Like, I mean, care about your eye or your nightmares? What do you think I'll do? Just stop loving you? Is that why you want me out of the bedroom? To make it, I don't know, easier for you to lose me?"

Will straightened up, though he still didn't look at Alex. "I don't want you out of the bedroom, I thought I'd made that clear." He did half a gesture of throwing something across the room.

"Yeah, you actually did." Alex paused, thinking about their fight after the elephant-incident. "So?"

"Nothing," said Will again, his voice cracking.

Alex sighed. "May I remind you of your words in the car earlier: 'We've got to stop lying to each other.' You really expect me to believe you when you say 'nothing' in that tone?"

And for the first time since he woke up from his nightmare, Will looked at Alex with his tousled hair, pillow dents on the side of his face and the 'I love beer'-T-shirt he'd gotten from Cohen for his last birthday.

"It's not going to go away," said Will quietly.

Alex rolled his eyes. "Yes, it will."

Will pointed at his blind eye. "This won't."

"I don't care how you look. Yes, I used to years ago, when it was still new and I got horny just thinking about the possibility of you." Will smiled slightly. "But we've gone past that a long time ago. I've seen you snort up hot chocolate through your nose as you tripped over the kitchen threshold. I've seen you with a runny nose and bloodshot eyes, coughing mucus into a paper towel in a really disgusting kind of way."

"No one looks good when they're sick. You don't either," said Will.

"Exactly my point. We've gone past the looking good is enough stage. I mean you're still hot most of the time, but that's not all it's about. So, no I don't care about your eye either. I don't care about any of it."

"But-"

"No 'but'. Stop thinking up excuses. I still love you and I still want you and I want to stop being afraid of touching you because I don't know how you'll react. Please let me touch you."

Will looked stunned and before he realised that he had nodded, Alex stepped closer and placed a quick kiss on his mouth before hugging him. He smelled like toothpaste, aloe vera shower gel and himself and his body was warm and comfortable.

"If you tell either Ruth, Abby or Cohen that I just said that I will throw out your favourite books," said Alex, his lips tickling the skin between shoulder and neck. Will smiled and then he remembered what he'd actually meant with 'it's not going to go away'.

25

The next morning, Alex woke up to loud cluttering in the kitchen. The bed on the other side was empty, but Alex remembered how they'd hugged again for the first time since Will had come back and it didn't really matter. Will was a morning person anyway. When he thought about it, it was actually a good sign.

By the time he'd taken a shower and dressed in his comfy jeans and a black t-shirt, the cluttering around the kitchen had stopped and the house was quiet. Alex checked to see whether Will was sitting at the dining table. The kitchen smelt like something had been burned and Alex shook his head in an amused way. But when Will wasn't in the living room either, he started to get a little worried. It was a few seconds before he noticed that the slide door leading out to the garden was slightly open. Walking around the sofa, Will came into view, standing on his stone and looking out towards to river. He was wearing a winter coat, which Alex was glad for. He nevertheless grabbed a blanket before stepping outside.

Will raised his eyebrow at him as he placed the blanket around his shoulders. Alex shrugged.

"Just to be safe," he said. Will's lungs chose that exact moment to make themselves known and he coughed, the coffee in the mug he was holding sloshing around dangerously.

"See."

Will grimaced. "Yes, mum."

"Did you eat whatever you burned?" asked Alex, trying – and failing – to hide a grin.

"Bacon. And yes. It wasn't too bad. The toast was worse. What's wrong with the toaster?" Will took a sip from the mug, the smell of freshly brewed coffee wafting over to Alex and making his mouth water.

"You have to be gentle with it. I think it has developed feelings. I'm going to make breakfast, do you still want anything?" Alex turned sideways, ready to go back inside.

Will shook his head, but still looked towards the river. "I'm good." And Alex couldn't resist, he rose to his tiptoes and pressed a kiss on Will's cheek. He didn't wait to see how Will reacted.

There was still coffee in the machine, enough for two more mugs, just the amount Alex almost always drank in the morning. He filled a mug and put some bread in the toaster, turning the knob to low heat. There was a sharp smell of burnt bread for a few seconds indicating the age and dirt level of their toaster, but by the time he had gotten the butter from the fridge it had turned into the delicious smell of crisp, warm toast. This was how he liked his mornings best. The taste of buttery toast on his tongue even before it was on the plate and a steaming mug of coffee to compliment it.

Five minutes later, he sat down in one of the old and very unstable garden chairs they owned, a plate with toast in one hand and a mug in the other. He placed the plate on his knees and looked up at Will.

"Sit down."

Will laughed. "Feeling small?" He went to get the second chair, though, and shortly after sat down next to Alex, the chair standing over his stone – not that he could see the river sitting down, but that didn't matter, it was still his stone. They sat in silence for a while, Alex eating his small breakfast. The toast became chewy rather quickly, because of the cold and the coffee stopped warming his hands after a few minutes, but he didn't want to give this up. If Will was staying outside, then so was he.

"I missed it."

"Missed what?" asked Alex. Will was still looking towards the general direction of the river, every now and then, turning his head slightly to look at the dry and cold bushes. Sometimes, a lonely leaf was blown through the air, lost and far away from all the other leaves that had left a few months earlier.

"Just sitting here, in this kind of weather, looking at the garden, the river. Just the nature. Afghanistan can be beautiful, especially the mountain ranges, but it's not the same. I really missed it." Will's voice was calm and quiet, as if he was sharing a secret that Alex had never heard before.

"It could be a bit warmer," said Alex, rubbing his hands together and blowing in the space between to warm them up.

"Yeah, a little bit," conceded Will. A swan flew overhead, calling once, its large wings shining blindingly white against the grey wall of clouds hiding the sun. They both watched it until it disappeared behind the trees, presumably having landed by the river to enjoy a lazy Saturday.

"Right, I'm gonna go inside. It's too cold." Alex jumped up and, putting the chair back in its original place, fled inside. He made a beeline for his mobile phone, quickly typing out a text before Will came back in.

Alex: We're talking.

Alex pocketed the phone and sat down on the couch, taking up one of the books. Will was still sitting outside and Alex was glad, he'd brought the extra blanket for him. As he sat on the couch, watching Will, he started to wonder whether Will had done that while he was at school working or whether Will had hidden himself away all day long, not once enjoying fresh air, as it had always seemed. Before he could think more about it, his phone buzzed.

Ruth: Awesome :) I quit my job and I think I got a boyfriend.

He wasn't quite sure how to react to that message over all. *Awesome* was not the answer he'd expected, but nor were the other two parts. He began to type out a message.

Alex: About fucking time, and you quit your job?

Just as he hit send, he realised who that potential boyfriend was.

Alex: Afterthought, how old is Ben?

He could imagine her rolling her eyes on the other side of town or wherever she was in that particular moment. It was just that Ben had seemed incredibly young, but maybe he himself was just old. Perhaps, he really was getting old – he felt it.

Ruth: Insignificantly younger than me. That's all you or our father for that matter need to know.

He silently agreed that his father should be kept out of it for now. He hadn't been a fan of Will in general, but even less so, it had seemed, when he found out that Will was working for the Royal British Army. If Ruth started dating a soldier as well, not to mention an injured one, well then, his father would probably start thinking his children were playing some strange games. It was only the end of February, but Alex was already dreading the Easter holidays when they got together for one of their rare family meetings. Christmas had been bearable because Eleanor had been there, but even if he did invite her for Easter too, he wasn't sure it was going to be as bearable this time. His father had never been a person of many phone calls, but the lack thereof since Will's return spoke volumes; and now his daughter brought along another injured soldier. It promised to be interesting.

Thinking of the holidays, he inquired after the other thing that had the potential to make Easter more horrible than usual.

Alex: Job?

He didn't have to wait long for a reply. He began to think that Ruth had not just quit today, but had been sitting on that information for some time.

Ruth: Hated it. On the look-out. Need a teacher?

Alex: No.

Ruth: ;_;

Alex: There'd be children involved.

Ruth: School secretary?

Alex: There'd still be children involved.

Ruth: Damn :(

Alex laughed. It wasn't just the absurd idea of Ruth working at a school or the conversation they'd just had; he felt better, genuinely better. He hadn't sat down to enjoy a book in weeks, he hadn't texted with his sister like that in weeks. With Will sitting where he felt most comfortable, it was easier for Alex to sit here and feel comfortable.

"What's so funny?" Alex turned to see Will standing just inside the living room. He turned to pull the slide door shut again, leaving the cold air outside.

"Um, Ruth. She needs a job and asked whether there was anything at school," said Alex.

Will dropped the blanket on the side arm of the couch and sat down. "She must be desperate."

"Well, I don't know when exactly she quit, so maybe she is," said Alex, smiling. He pulled one of his legs up onto the couch to get into a more comfortable position. This could be a really nice Saturday.

"Can I ask you something?" Could have been a really nice Saturday the way Will sounded.

"What is it?" asked Alex.

Will simply held up a piece of paper and it took Alex a few seconds to figure out what it was, but then he deciphered 'Dr. M. Khan' in the middle of the page and realised it was the list of psychologists Abby had given him.

"Did you ask Abby to make this list?" Will took it in both hands and looked at it thoughtfully.

"You know it's from Abby?" said Alex, glad that he didn't have to explain everything.

"I know her handwriting Alex. And I know your handwriting even better."

"I didn't ask her. I did tell her about that doctor and what he'd said and I think she agreed with him, so she went to have a look," explained Alex in a low voice. He hoped Will would see it as a good gesture, rather than an accusation or assumption about his mental state.

"What do you think? Do you agree with them as well?" Will fiddled with the paper and didn't look at Alex, whose sinking feeling returned as strong as ever. Every step they'd taken since yesterday afternoon was suddenly reversed again, simply because Will had found that stupid paper that he'd been too pre-occupied for to get rid of.

Alex took a deep breath. "I think it's your choice and no one can talk you into or out of it."

Will seemed to mull that answer over for some time before finally looking at Alex. "Very diplomatic answer," he said, a sarcastic undertone colouring the words. "What do you really think?"

Funnily enough, no one else had asked him that yet. "I still think that ultimately, it is your choice."

"But?" Will put the paper on the couch table and turned to Alex. He, on the other hand, wasn't sure that there was a *but*. Once he properly thought about it, however, he found that there was one.

"I feel selfish saying this, but I'd prefer if you talked to me rather than to some stranger. But it might help you, better than I could – with your nightmares." Alex held his breath as he waited for Will's reaction. There was no answer; Will simply took the paper again, looked at it, folded it up and put it back on the table. He pulled up his legs, squeezing his feet underneath Alex's thigh and leaning his head against the back rest.

"Read it to me," he said, looking at the book, still unopened in Alex's hands. Alex looked at it – *Another world* by Pat Barker. He had read the back cover, he knew what it was about, and thought that perhaps they ought to pick a different one.

"One of the themes is World War One," said Alex, fighting the urge to get up, chuck the book out and get a new one. Why did he have to pick this one from the pile, out of all the books lying around?

"I know, I've read Pat Barker before. Read it to me." Will nodded reassuringly, before closing his eyes. Opening the book, Alex turned to the first chapter, cleared his throat and began to read.

26

They skipped lunch, having biscuits and tea at around 3 o'clock and an early dinner at 5:30. Alex's voice grew hoarse as the day progressed, his mouth drying up more quickly than a few hours earlier, but he simply paused to take a drink and continued. Will stayed by his side, resenting having to get up to go to the toilet or to have something to eat, but both his bladder and Alex insisted. He liked sitting on the couch, listening to Alex's voice while the world around them grew dark. It was strangely comforting.

Once they had finished their dinner, Will was ready to go back into the living room to continue being read to, thinking he could do that all night, when the doorbell rang. Alex answered it, while Will cleared away the rest of the dishes.

"Hey stranger."

Cohen had his hands in his jeans pocket and didn't look like he was about to rush over to Will to hug him. With a pang of guilt, Will realised that Cohen probably had no idea about his hospital visit.

"How are you? Temper smoothed over?" asked Cohen, looking at Will intently, as if he was waiting for an explosion and didn't want to miss the moment when he should run for it.

"Yeah. Hi."

Alex squeezed past them and picked up the dishes that Will hadn't dried and put away yet. "So, back from London? How was it?"

Cohen shrugged. "Busy and boring. They're all money-loving idiots down there. Every time I'm there, I get why you didn't want to step in your father's shoes, Alex."

Alex raised an eyebrow, a reaction that made Will smile. "Good to know we agree on something."

Cohen shuffled closer, every now and then looking at Will, still waiting for some sign that he wasn't wanted.

"A bird called Abby told me it was much more exciting here."

Will scoffed and Alex said exactly what he was thinking. "I wouldn't call six days in hospital exciting."

"More like depressing," added Will quietly.

"Then there's only one thing we can do-"

"No, Cohen. We're not going to the pub. Will's on antibiotics anyway. He's not allowed to drink alcohol," said Alex, adopting a voice that usually only his students had the pleasure of hearing.

"He can drink cranberry juice. Come on, guys, you kind of promised last week, Alex, and I haven't done anything with my bro since he got back except yell after him in the middle of the night."

Will had always admired how Cohen managed to say the right things in order to push the right buttons. If he kept going, he would initiate a whole three-week guilt trip with stops at Disneyland and the Chinese Wall.

"Besides, after a week in hospital, the only place to be is a pub." Cohen grinned at them, arms thrown open wide. Alex was shaking his head in a disbelieving kind of way, but Will couldn't help but think that he owed Cohen. He owed Cohen a night out and he owed him an apology, something that was best delivered in the form of a night out.

"Okay."

"Okay?" asked Alex, completely taken aback.

"Yeah, okay." Will bit his lip. Together, he and Cohen waited for Alex's response.

"You're sure?" he asked. He was watching Will, trying to read him.

"I'm sure," he said, though he knew he didn't fully sound like it. Cohen clapped his hands together.

"Brilliant. Grab your coats and let's go."

27

Heads turned as they entered the pub and headed for the bar. It wasn't the pub down the street, Cohen having insisted on going somewhere new. The patrons were not from their immediate neighbourhood. Will wasn't sure he liked it. Around 30 pairs of eyes watched them, following the scar rather than them as a group and Will found he developed a nervous blinking tick. He coughed once and it was almost funny how Alex was immediately at his side to ask if he was okay. He nodded imperceptibly. Before they even sat down, Cohen had already begun flirting with the barmaid.

"Can your gorgeous self get us two lagers and a cranberry juice for this guy?" he said. The barmaid smiled at him, not even checking who'd be drinking the other two drinks.

"No cranberry juice, where do you get that from?" said Will.

"Hot Fuzz. Great movie. What do you want then?" Only as Cohen focused his attention on Will did the barmaid also look up. Her smile faltered as she saw Will's face and Will had to say diet coke twice before she woke up out of her trance.

"Yes, sorry, two lagers and a diet coke." She turned to prepare the drinks, not even looking at Cohen anymore.

"Yeah, she kind of lost her appeal," said Cohen, not sounding very disappointed. "So, Will: Hospital didn't suit you, did it? You look kind of terrible."

"Does hospital suit anybody?" asked Alex, nodding at the barmaid as she placed the lager in front of him. She was still gaping at Will, unable to avert her eyes, while he avoided looking at her entirely.

"Thanks, love," said Cohen, forcefully waving the 20-pound note in front of her face.

"Right." She took the note and went to the register.

"Definitely lost her appeal. Anyway, hospitals, I've always wondered about the contradiction they present. I mean, they are supposed to help people, heal them and so on, but actually you feel worse while you're in them. What's up with that?"

If Will didn't know that Cohen could be serious, intelligent and almost frighteningly considerate if and when he wanted to, he would never have become his friend, let alone one of his best friends. Most of the time Will just sat there with an exasperated smile on his lips, an expression Alex had over time copied from him, while Cohen had learned to ignore it and just keep talking. Usually, however, he kept on talking about more nonsense until something actually triggered a response from someone – not this time.

"How are you, Will? Seriously!"

Will glanced at Alex, saw the curiosity in his eyes and the fear of a negative answer. "Better."

Relief flitted across Alex's face and Will even believed his own answer. Cohen's hand on his shoulder made him look the other side again. "Good. I'm glad. Maybe the hospital trip did some good after all. To the hospital." Cohen raised his glass in a mock salute. Will sighed, but then followed suit.

"I thought you hated that place," whispered Alex, smirking.

"I did. Shut up!" replied Will, clinking glasses with Cohen first.

As he reached around to toast with Alex, a strange hand clapped his shoulder. "Oi, mate. You Irish? Did the IRA do that to you?" Loud laughter rang in Will's ears. He couldn't see who was laughing and had their hand on his shoulder, they were standing to his left - in his blind spot. He felt a twinge of frustration at that thought, but even he had to admit to himself that he did indeed now have a blind spot. He'd never liked it when people stood right behind him – the only perimeter where you couldn't see anything. It gave him goose bumps and the urge to lash out. That perimeter had gotten bigger since his accident and less vision meant less control. Whoever had laughed, had picked the perfect spot for full control. Will would have to turn in his seat to gain it back.

He sensed both Alex and Cohen shifting, turning before he could and placing one of the legs in front of them on the floor, ready to jump up and do something that would get them kicked out of the pub and into a police cell.

"It wasn't IRA, thanks," said Alex.

The drunk stranger removed his hand and Will chose that moment to face him, to see him. They were back on his terms.

"Woah woahoho, you look fierce man," laughed the drunk stranger, holding out his fist for Will to bump it. The other patrons were raising their heads and stopping their conversations in order to watch the confrontation, for Will was sure it was going to turn into one.

Both drunk men looked as if they'd been looking for someone to fight with all evening. Their breaths smelled of beer, their hair was combed back or hidden underneath a baseball cap and their tracksuits looked stained and well-used. Will wasn't sure they were really old enough to be drinking in the first place, but it was pointless to worry about that.

"How did'ya get it then?" asked the first one, adjusting his baseball cap.

"Like he's going to tell you." To Will's surprise, Cohen was already fully standing, beating the drunkards in size only by a few centimetres. Will placed a hand on Cohen's chest to warn him.

The second guy now spoke up for the first time, nudging his friend. "Ey, he's one of'em Tern Hill soldiers, I bet 'e is."

Baseball cap guy looked very interested in that. "I see, you got yourself blown up in Iran or somefin'."

"We're not at war with Iran, but if you want to start one, you're welcome to join up. I'm sure the Army would appreciate your well-informed opinion." Neither of the drunkards missed out on the cynicism in Will's voice.

"Oh, he's bein' fresh with us." Baseball cap stepped closer, perhaps hoping Will would back down, but alcohol made the most intelligent people stupid and blind-sided. "So, ya go off to that war that nobody wants-" "Waste of fuckin' money. Our money!" –"yeah, waste of fuckin' money, an' then ya get yerself blown up. Enjoyin' our life, livin' off benefits, are we?"

"What the fuck are you talking about?" asked Cohen. Behind him, the barmaid was getting nervous and shouted for the manager.

"'E goes off, shoots some poor folk who done nothin' an' he comes back with half a face an' neva has to raise a hand eva again, gets his money for bein' a murderer. Lazy murderer! That's what 'e is." Both boys were now looking at Will provocatively, waiting for him to deal the first blow, so that they could blame him in the end. It was Alex's hand on his back that stopped him, though the anger curled inside of him like a tumour waiting to grow and grow and consume everything.

"For god's sake, leave him alone. He's a hero, who's had enough hardship. He doesn't have to deal with you idiots." A man in his mid-40s with strands of grey in his hair, yelled the boys. They turned and gave him the finger.

"Shut up, Grandpa. So, what do ya do, huh?"

It was ridiculous, Will knew it was ridiculous. The manager was standing behind the bar, threatening to call the police, the mid-40s man was complaining to his date about the youth of today by the looks of it and Cohen looked about as ready to fight as anyone could. Will's anger, however, had been replaced by a sinking feeling as soon as the boy had asked his question. Every angry thought, every insult left his body and all he could think was that they were actually right. He looked at Alex and then at the door and Alex got the hint, but then he made the mistake of placing his hand on Will's neck like he usually did; because Will loved it and Alex only wanted him to feel better.

"OMG, he's fuckin' queer too. I didn't know ya guys could be murderers too, I thought it's only rainbows and bu'erflies up yer arses." The boy's voice filled the whole room and echoed around Will's head. Alex had almost steered him past them, Cohen had walked around on the other side and was now leading the way. He imagined the manager already breathing a sigh of relief, but no, Will couldn't get that voice out of his head. *Murderer, queer, lazy, murderer, murderer...*

Murderer.

His fist connected with the solar plexus, knocking the wind out of the first boy. The second sprang into action and was stopped with a well-placed blow to the nose, breaking it immediately. He stumbled backwards, while Will slammed his fist into the side of the first boy's head, knocking him out cold. The other one looked up at him, stunned, and didn't dare attack again.

He leaned down, speaking quietly. "That should teach you not to attack a soldier. Faugh a ballagh, you cunt."

All around, pub patrons were staring, some standing as if they'd wanted to help. Cohen and Alex were right behind Will. The pub door was swinging on its hinges; its creaking filling the uncomfortable silence.

The manager came around the bar. "Get out!" he said to the boys, phone in hand, though he hadn't called the police yet. He turned towards Will. "All of you."

Will could hear Cohen drawing breath to say something, but he didn't want to be there to hear what it was. He just wanted to leave.

The cold air hit his face and numbed his thoughts for a second. He appreciated it. He turned left, heading in the direction of their house, but two streets on he turned right again. Footsteps were following him hurriedly, though neither Alex nor Cohen made any other sound.

He reached the river bank in under ten minutes, walking as far as the old oak tree before he stopped and sat down. His legs were hanging over the edge again. A duck cautiously swam closer, in hope of a late supper, but it quickly left again after realising that Will wasn't going to comply.

"Will?"

At the sound of Alex's voice, everything drained out of him, the anger, the aggression and left were only the words. He didn't want to cry in front of Cohen. He'd never cried in front of Cohen. Leaning forward slightly, he placed his head in his hands.

Alex and Cohen must have had some kind of silent conversation, because it was a minute before Cohen placed a hand on Will's head, gently ruffling his hair.

"I'll leave you to it and I'll call you." Cohen hesitated, as if waiting for a reply. Will wasn't ready to speak yet, and he hoped Cohen would understand that. "Don't let them get to you, yeah?"

Will nodded, even though it was a lie. It was too late for it to become true. Whether Cohen believed him or not, he removed his hand and slowly walked away. Will waited until he could no longer hear any footsteps, before raising his head again. He could sense Alex standing to his right, his feet just visible in the corner of his eyes if he strained his vision.

"Sit down."

Alex didn't wait to be asked twice. "They are getting to you, aren't they?"

Will wanted to pretend, so he shook his head. To their right, two ducks began quacking loudly, one chasing the other across the water. Will watched them and wondered how his fight must have looked like to the on-lookers. Heroic or foolish? He should have walked away.

"I should have walked away." Will was banging his feet against the stone wall, producing a dull sound which echoed back to them. *Thud thud.*

Alex nodded. "Yeah, you should have. But I'm glad you didn't. They were idiots."

"Doesn't mean they deserved it," said Will. *Thud thud thud thud.*

"No, I think they did," said Alex. He placed a hand on Will's knee and again, it felt like the calming anchor that put him back on the ground.

"I need to do something," he said, determined.

"Do what?"

"Find a job or education. Maybe find a psychologist. Maybe I should."

Alex removed his hand, and immediately Will felt vulnerable again. He wasn't sure whether he wanted to have a confrontation, but he knew Alex wouldn't just accept this uncontested.

"Because of them. They were asking for it and they deserved it." A bitterness resounded in these words, and Will remembered that this hadn't been the first time for them to hear snide remarks or outright insults about their sexuality. It left a sour taste in their minds that came back every now and then like mould.

"But would I have done it at another time, with different circumstances?" asked Will, already knowing the answer. He simply wanted to remind Alex of the answer.

"No, you wouldn't have."

Three swans were swimming past them, turning their heads for a glimpse of these two humans, making sure that this wasn't an invasion of their territory. They settled on the other side of the river, feeling safe enough to comb their feathers with their beaks. Will wanted to stay here all night and watch them, but the cold was starting to creep underneath his jacket and he knew that it was the best thing to do when Alex suggested they should go home.

Halfway home, Will gave in to the urge of holding Alex's hand. The surprise on Alex's face was both amusing and sad at the same time, but Will didn't comment on it. He just wanted to enjoy the silent walk home, the comfortable feeling of the warm hand and soft skin.

28

That night was bad again. The nightmare must have probably been so violent that Will lashed, one of his legs kicking Alex in the shin and his arm hitting his shoulder forcefully. Alex had a hard time waking him up and when he did, Will simply got up and went into the bathroom. For half an hour, Alex listened to the shower running, but having put fresh sheets on the bed already and having had only 3 hours of sleep so far, his eyes fell shut before the shower stopped.

It didn't get better the next night, nor the next. By Tuesday, Alex's lack of sleep made him so tired that he needed three energy drinks to get through the day. At the end of the day, he walked to his car as if in a daze, rummaging for his car keys and cursing the size of his bag and the amount of paper in it.

"Looking for these?"

He looked up and saw Abby standing against his car, dangling his keys in front of her. She looked wary.

"Yes, actually. When did you take them?"

She walked towards him. "Technically, I didn't. Gareth is a nice kid and for some reason you're his favourite teacher. It wasn't hard to persuade him."

Astonished, Alex shook his head. "You persuaded a 17-year-old student of ours to steal car keys out of a teacher's bag?"

She smirked. "Wasn't as easy as you might think. I told him it was his moral obligation."

"Ah, you shouldn't have done that," said Alex, laughing now. He could imagine how that conversation went.

"Well, yeah, I know that now. He started this philosophical discussion with me. He mentioned utilitarianism, though I don't really know in which context. After about two minutes, I wasn't able to follow him anymore. So, in a way, he persuaded himself, because he sort of talked himself towards the solution of helping me get the keys."

"Yeah, he does that. Happens in History as well. It's fascinating to watch," said Alex, yawning widely.

"Anyway, he asked me to beg you not to punish him, he thought he was helping." Abby pleaded with her eyes.

"What was he helping with anyway?" asked Alex, narrowing his eyes to make it seem like he was angry.

"You can't drive like that. I'm amazed you made it to school this morning. Even the janitor noticed how tired you are, and you know how he usually doesn't 'see' things. When's the last time you slept properly?"

Alex walked past her towards the passenger side of the car. "Christmas Day."

Abby unlocked the car, glaring at Alex across the car roof. "Alex! Seriously, when?"

Alex just looked at her with a deadpan stare and eventually, it dawned on her.

"Seriously? Christmas? Oh my god. I mean, really?" Abby was so shocked she forgot to open the car.

"Well, if by properly you mean, sleeping through the night for approximately 8 hours straight, then yes, Christmas Day. 'Cause after that, Eleanor went home and on the same day, we heard of Will's injury. Then I didn't sleep because of worry, and since Will's been back, I haven't slept properly either, again, because I'm too worried or because he keeps waking me up with his nightmares. Even last week when he was in hospital, I couldn't sleep properly. I kept thinking about him, or even dreaming about him."

"Jesus." She dropped the heavy bag from her shoulders and walked around the car.

"Abby, it's-"

"Shut up." She pulled him down into a hug and he let her. "I'm sorry about our fight, I never wanted that."

"I know."

She squeezed him even tighter. "Ruth said you don't know what to do either, but neither do we. We just want to help and I thought if he-"

"Okay, stop," said Alex, gently pulling out of the hug and holding Abby at arms' length. "I shouldn't have reacted that way, and you were kind of right. He's actually thinking about it."

"Is he?" She smiled at that information, looking pleased.

"He found the list and things happened and-"

"The pub thing?" she interrupted.

Alex threw up his arms in despair. "Bloody hell. Every time I talk to one of you, you guys already know everything. It feels like you're spying on us. Do you guys call each other up every evening to exchange the newest happenings with Will and me?"

Abby opened her mouth, closed it, opened it again and paused. "Yeah, pretty much. Maybe not every night, and we don't always talk on the phone, sometimes it's just a text or an-"

"Abby, just take me home," said Alex. She nodded and went back to the driver's door, unlocking the car this time. Alex threw his heavy bag onto the backseat, where it was closely followed by Abby's equally heavy bag.

Abby put the key in the ignition, but didn't turn it yet. "Just to be clear, we're really just worried. About both of you."

"And I'm sure at some point, when I'm less tired and less annoyed by everything, I'll appreciate it," said Alex, leaning his head against the back of the car seat and closing his eyes. "Now, kind chauffeur, take me home."

Only when they arrived in front of his house, did Alex realise that Abby couldn't very well drive away with his car and would have a hard time getting home with buses. As it turned out, though, she'd dealt with that particular problem on her own already.

"Matt is coming around to pick me up. He's been so busy lately, I think he enjoys just spending a few minutes in the car with me. He was positively beaming this morning, when he drove me to school. It's kind of cute," she said, smiling shyly. Her cheeks blushed, making her look even more beautiful than usual.

"Two years married and still in love like on the first day," said Alex, though he wasn't really mocking her. He'd always liked watching Matt and Abby together.

"It's only been two years. Let's talk again in twenty."

As soon as they entered the house, Will walked into the hallway, dressed in sweat pants and a rather tight T-shirt. The pants hung so low that his hip bones were visible underneath the shirt; like sharp rocks on a smooth plain. Alex had to tear his eyes away forcefully.

"Apparently, I'm too tired to drive myself, or so Abby says." Alex rolled his eyes in mock- exasperation, but Will didn't smile.

"Hi, Abby."

There was a pause that could be described as awkward. Without saying anything, Abby knew how well-informed Will was about the origin of the list of psychologists. She moved past Alex right up to Will, positioning herself in front of him like she would do with students when they either needed a telling-off or a particularly intense bit of motivation.

"I only thought that you might want to give it a try," she said. She sounded small, smaller than usual and Alex wondered what she was thinking.

"I know," said Will and then he looked up and straight at Alex. "And I did."

Alex was taken aback, not by the confession, but by the look in Will's eyes. It was hard to decipher, as if Will wanted to tell him something that he couldn't say out loud, but Alex couldn't grasp it.

"You did? When?"

"This morning," said Will, his voice not quite sounding like his own.

"How was it?" asked Abby, abruptly stopping the whirl of thoughts in Alex's head. For a few seconds he'd forgotten she was still here. It seemed, so had Will. He swallowed and slowly lowered his head to answer her.

"Weird."

Abby put her hand on his arm in a comforting gesture. "Well, it's bound to be, when it's the first time. It will probably take some sessions. Come on, I'll make us a cuppa." Squeezing his arm, she went into the kitchen, leaving them alone.

Alex waited for Will to speak, giving him the chance to say what he wanted to say. Will swallowed again. "I've already filled out the forms and handed them in. The army will pay for it. They actually recommended him. So, don't worry about the money."

Alex shook his head. "I wasn't thinking about that." He was still waiting, there was something else, he knew there was something else.

"Tea's ready." Abby popped her head around the corner and smiled at them. "Come on, Matt'll probably be here in twenty minutes and I want some boys time."

29

He lay in bed, staring at the ceiling and listened to the running shower. Alex preferred showering in the mornings; late night showers always meant he was extremely exhausted. Will felt guilty as he was the one keeping him awake most of the time. He had to think back at what Dr. Khan had said twenty minutes into their sessions.

"If something wants out and you won't let it, it will find a different way."

That he wasn't sleeping very well was clear to anyone who looked at the dark shadows under his eyes and to someone who'd had dealings with soldiers before it must be a natural conclusion that nightmares were at the core of the problem. The thought of talking about it, however, haunted him just as much. Half the time he'd felt sick while talking to Dr. Khan. He hadn't even really been able to answer the question why he was there. He hadn't been quite sure; it wasn't just the incident at the pub, it wasn't just Abby's list and Alex's little unconscious nudges - which Alex would never admit to even if he had been aware of them – like the way the piece of paper with the names on kept reappearing in places or how after *Another World* Alex began reading Pat Barker's *Regeneration*, set in an asylum, a psychologist being one of the protagonist. But he also didn't feel like he really wanted to talk to someone. It frightened him, and the one thing he didn't need was something else to have nightmares about.

The shower stopped and for a moment Will thought about pretending to be asleep, but after the progress they'd had it would probably give Alex the wrong signs. So, instead he sat up straighter, stretched out his legs and pretended to be reading.

Alex came out a few minutes later – Will actually having managed to read half a page -, hair standing on end and a towel wrapped around his hips. He went towards the cupboard taking out new briefs.

"Those are mine."

"Write your name in them," teased Alex as usual and Will's stomach flipped once.

"One day I will."

Alex laughed. "You say that every time. We need to put on a machine tomorrow." He turned off the light, leaving only the bedside lamps still burning. It threw off Will's vision again, changing his mood instantly. He heard the rustle of the bed, meaning Alex was settling under the duvet. Once he was done puffing up the pillows and punching his duvet to get comfortable, there was a moment of silence.

Will knew Alex was working up the nerve to ask him something, but he also found he'd rather not initiate that conversation.

"Do you want to talk about today?" asked Alex, disrupting the silence.

Will wished he would have just come out with it rather than ask that. Given the option, he just couldn't say yes. "Not really."

"Will you go to him again?"

Will sighed, more out of relief than anything else. He appreciated the simplicity of the question. He could deal with that, he could answer it – could even please Alex while answering it. "Yes, I think so."

"Okay."

Suddenly, the bed rustled and Will felt soft lips lightly pressed against his cheek, right underneath his left eye. It almost tickled. He turned his head abruptly, but still didn't really see Alex, not his face anyway.

"Good night," said Alex, followed by the click of the lamp as he turned it off. Still stunned, Will slowly slid down the bed and settled into his pillow. He clicked his lamp, filling the room with darkness, while the feeling of Alex's lips still lingered.

He lay there tensely, listening to Alex's breathing, waiting for it to slow down, to develop the rhythm of a sleeping person, except it didn't.

"Alex?"

"Yeah?" The speed of Alex's reaction told Will that he'd just been waiting for it and Will decided to not say what Alex was probably expecting.

"We should change the sides of the bed tomorrow. You should sleep on the window side from now on."

The pause told Will that his words had had the desired effect.

"Are you sure?" asked Alex after a minute.

"Yes."

There was quite some tumult on the other side of the bed, telling him that Alex was turning over, which he never could do quietly or without much movement. He always seemed to be adjusting the entire bed to suit his sleeping comfort when he was turning on his side. It made Will smile.

"You know," whispered Alex once he'd stopped moving, "you were kind of hot today in those sweat pants and that T-shirt. I liked it."

Will laughed softly, his face growing warm at the same time. "Is that why you kissed me on the cheek?" he said. "Like a five-year-old."

"Shut up," said Alex, amused.

"The cheek, Alex."

Anything else he wanted to say was drowned by a kiss that was far away from the chasteness of the first one. Alex had turned Will's head towards him and pressed their lips together, trapping Will's upper lip between his own. The surprise caused Will to leave his eyes open, watching Alex's face; the pleased look on it, the closed eyes positively screaming at Will that Alex was really enjoying this. So, he closed his eyes as well and kissed him back.

They stayed like that for some time, simply relishing the fact that they were kissing again at all. Alex's thumb was caressing Will's face, playing with his right earlobe every now and then.

Will shifted, moving closer to Alex, yearning to feel the warmth. Their legs touched and then Alex moved his in between Will's, their bodies aligning perfectly like always and Will realised how much he'd missed that.

Alex broke the kiss, but only so he could lower his lips to Will's neck, biting down on his collarbone. Will's fingers gripped the still clammy hair tight, guiding Alex a little bit higher to that spot he loved the most.

God! How he'd missed it!

His hips jerked up a little bit and Alex moaned into his neck, one of his hands sliding down along Will's side, tucking up his T-shirt as they reached their destination. Alex's hand was warm against his skin and it felt like a steaming cup of hot chocolate after a long day out in the deepest snow.

Will moaned quietly and it was that moment that his lungs decided that they'd had enough excitement. It was a slow rise to the top, he could feel it build up like the orgasm he was looking forward to having. And just as Alex was moving in to continue the kiss, his lungs convulsed violently and he more or less shoved Alex off.

"Fuck, Will, shit." Alex scrambled out of bed while Will raised his torso to take the pressure off his lungs.

"Please." His cough was now a low rumbling sound, filling the room like a thundering drum. The usual wheezing sound was hiding somewhere in between, high and barely discernible. "Please don't say 'fuck'."

Then there was an inhaler in his hand, the lamp was back on and Alex was sitting at his side, rubbing his back as he inhaled deeply. His lungs hurt slightly and he still coughed as if trying to get rid of an annoying fly.

"Well, that obviously was a bit too much excitement," said Alex, trying hard to make it sound like a very amusing joke. "We can try that again another time."

But Will didn't feel like laughing, not now, not after this, not when for once he'd gotten past his horrible feeling of inadequacy. Suddenly, he couldn't quite bear having Alex next to him, rubbing his back. He scrambled across the bed and hurried into the bathroom, locking the door behind him. Except then he had to look at himself in the mirror. Frustration, anger rose up inside of him and he threw his stupid inhaler at the mirror, where it simply rebounded and skidded towards the toilet bowl.

He slid to the ground with his back against the door and began to cry. He knew Alex could hear him on the other side, but he didn't care.

Fuck that bomb, why did it have to be chlorine gas? Why couldn't it have been a normal bomb, an RPG bomb, a grenade, anything else? Why gas?

He heard Alex calling his name once, but didn't react.

He didn't know how much time had passed before he finally decided to open the door again and go to bed, but Alex was fast asleep, lying on the side of the bed closer to the window. His right hand was now on Will's side, as if waiting for him to fill it. He climbed in and placed Alex's hand on his chest and imagined it having healing powers.

30

Neither commented on that night; Alex pressed a kiss against Will's forehead the next morning, simply as a sign that this wasn't the last of it.

Nor did they try again and consciously or unconsciously, Will wasn't wearing that tight T-shirt anymore.

Abby picked Alex up every day now, saying that he could sleep some more in the car.

By the end of March, the weather outside was warmer than their bed, or at least it felt that way to Will. They touched and it wasn't in any way like the distance they had at the beginning, but it was almost never more than Alex's hand on his chest or a small good night kiss. When Will turned off the light, the inhaler was always in sight and he almost always fell asleep with feelings of resentment towards it.

Slowly but surely, the sun was coming out more frequently and with it, the first crocuses. Here and there, they were showing their purple or white heads and the stems of daffodils started coming out of the earth as well. Whenever Will now went outside to eat breakfast, he simply took a thin blanket to put over his shoulder. In his head, Will was already planning the organisation of the garden. A few rose bushes needed to be planted, and maybe one day they could consider a cherry tree.

While he looked at the garden, he usually thought of something Dr. Khan had said during their frequent sessions. Often, he made a cup of tea and went to Alex's small office, crammed full of books and lesson plans. There he opened the laptop, where he spent his time until Alex was due to come home.

31

It didn't happen, simply didn't – not to him anyway. His mobile was never on mute, granted, but it didn't have to be. He only gave this number to friends and family and they all knew not to bother him before 3 o'clock; the students did all the bothering he could take until that time.

Nevertheless, he now owed his students muffins as his phone had gone off in the middle of class; worse, in the middle of a student presentation. He had looked at the display very quickly while turning it off and Eleanor's name glaring back at him opened up an abyss in his stomach. As soon as the lesson had been over and he'd more or less kicked his students out of the room and locked it he had turned his mobile back on and was now dialling Eleanor's number.

"Oh god, Alex, I'm sorry, you were in class, weren't you? I wasn't thinking," apologised Eleanor before he had a chance to say hello.

"Don't worry about it. Is everything okay?" The fact that she'd apologised for disrupting his lesson made his pulse slow down again. She wouldn't be apologising if some true emergency had happened.

"Yes, yes, at least I hope it will be. I was just so flustered I forgot I wasn't supposed to call you-"

"It's fine," interrupted Alex. He'd rather have information than another apology. "What happened?"

Eleanor sighed; not exactly a good sign. "Well, a sergeant from the Royal Irish Army called me to invite me to the homecoming briefing they will be holding for the returning Operation Herrick 13 troops. You know, they're coming back in April."

Alex was momentarily confused. "Why are they calling you?"

"Well, either they have simply forgotten that Will is already home or they think that it might still be useful for us, I don't know."

Alex sat down behind his desk. He was pretty sure they'd simply forgotten, considering it was March 31st. "So what does this involve?"

"It's this homecoming briefing informing us, family and friends, about the four stages of decompression, normalisation, the stress of integrating back into society etc."

Alex laughed. "Yeah, they're a bit fucking late for that. Sorry, bad language, sorry."

"That's okay. I feel the same." She hesitated, yet another loud sigh reaching Alex's ear.

"What?"

"There're also the parades through Tern Hill and Market Drayton, and technically Belfast as well."

Alex remembered the homecoming parades. Most of Tern Hill and Market Drayton were up on their feet, cheering on the returning soldiers who marched to the beat of the military band, showing off their colours. Will had always been incredibly proud to be able to march with these soldiers; had always said it felt like having a gang of brothers taking over these small towns.

But now Alex wasn't so sure how Will would think about these parades.

"It's his decision," said Alex, because no matter how he put it, it was. Alex might have some claim over the whole going to a psychologist thing because Will was bound to be talking about them as well, but going to the parades or not was Will's decision – whether either he or Eleanor liked it or not.

"I wish he wouldn't. This can't be good for him. I mean, even if he's going to that psychologist now, I'm not sure it's good if he's marching with some of his colleagues in that parade knowing full well that he's not going back into service." Eleanor sounded worried and Alex knew she was biting her lips as was her nervous habit.

"Yeah, I don't think so - Hang on! No, wait, I don't even want to know who told you about the psychologist," said Alex, banging his head onto the desk in exasperation. They were worse than the CIA.

"Ruth gives me regular updates," said Eleanor.

"Of course she does," said Alex, his head still on the desk.

"My own son doesn't talk to me, though I can forgive him for that, and you only give me answers when I call you first. I hate to be the nagging mum here, but you two are not exactly A star sons."

A pang of guilt made Alex raise his head again. "Would it help to know that we're battling with our own problems?"

"Not really, Alex," she said. "It just makes me worry even more."

Alex sighed. He was fumbling with one of his pens, clicking and tapping it – one of the more annoying habits that he had to get rid of as a teacher. "It's getting better, *we* are getting better. Really."

"Good to know. And you know, maybe the parade isn't the worst idea. He'd see Andrew again, for sure," added Eleanor.

Alex had to relent to that. Andrew had been Will's right hand from the moment he'd moved into the barracks for the first time. They did their first mission together in Kosovo and survived it without a scratch. They'd both been keen on Afghanistan, signing up for it as soon as word about Operation Herrick 13 was out. Having Andrew back in Tern Hill might actually really be a good thing.

"So, are you going to that briefing?" asked Alex. He remembered the last one: while it had been interesting, he hadn't been sure he'd felt really prepared for the homecoming. He definitely hadn't been prepared for this homecoming, but he was also sure that however good the briefing might have been, it could never have adequately prepared for what was to come.

"No, it's too late and it's not like he's coming home to me. But do tell him about the parades before he hears it from somebody else; and hug him from me. And call! Once a week would be nice."

"But we have talked once a month, I think that's an achievement on my part," said Alex, hoping he would make Eleanor laugh. In addition to worried, she also sounded sad and Alex had never liked her sounding sad. She sounded that way when she talked about her late husband and he didn't want to have to associate that tone with Will and himself.

"If you say so," she answered and he imagined he could hear a hint of a laugh. "I'll talk to you soon, love."

"Bye Eleanor."

Alex pressed the red phone button and dropped the phone on the desk. He rubbed his eyes but jerked his head up when he heard a sharp rap on the window pane of the class room door. In front of the door stood his Year 12 History class, waiting to be let in. Alex looked at the watch and saw that the lesson had started 9 minutes ago.

"Ah dammit." Cursing to himself, he stood up and unlocked the door. "Sorry about that. Come in, come in."

"That's okay, Mr. Benson. You haven't given us any marks in the last two months, so we forgive you," said the petite Sarah, smiling broadly at him. Simon pushed past her, furiously whispering: "Ssh, don't tell him. I don't think he noticed until you just told him."

Alex cursed again, silently this time. He really hadn't noticed, and he really needed to change something about that – and pretend that the lack of marks had been fully intentional.

32

Parents' night lasted till 8:30 p.m. and Alex had a hard time concentrating; his thoughts were with Will at home and his lack of sleep was doing the rest. Most of the parents had pity in their eyes, their children probably having told them about his current circumstances. More than ever he felt the immense amount of scrutiny that teachers were always under.

Matt picked both him and Abby up, throwing a chocolate bar at each of them. "Have a treat. How nasty was it?"

Abby sighed as she leaned back into the passenger seat, while Alex simply stared out of the window. He was knackered and just wanted to go home and have a cup of tea.

"It was alright, until Mrs. MacPherson walked in," said Abby. "I was hoping she'd stay away since Toby's marks have gone up. He's a C to B student now, which is a lot better than before. But obviously still not good enough and I should do something about it. I'm a bad teacher and she has to send him to tutoring to make up for my lack of competence."

"What a b." Matt was shaking his head in astonishment.

"She's always been a massive b. and she will continue being one. Tonight was nice in comparison to what she did last year. I just feel sorry for the kid. Toby is so nice, but I'm not sure he's cut out for A-levels. Matt, where are you going?" asked Abby suddenly.

"Home," he replied. "Where your dinner is waiting, you know."

"That's really sweet of you, but we've got Alex in the car. You should have turned right three crossroads ago."

"Oh god, sorry, I wasn't thinking," said Matt, smiling at Alex apologetically via the rear view mirror.

Alex grinned half-heartedly. "Don't worry, looking forward to dinner, are we?"

Matt winked at him, while Abby reached over to pat his knee. "He always makes my favourite on parents' night."

"I bet he does."

Abby picked up a packet of tissues and threw it at Alex, having almost no effect at all. Both he and Matt started laughing. "Oi, watch it, you two. I'm in a sour mood and you know what I can do."

"Sorry, honey," said Matt, immediately sobering up.

"That dinner better be bloody perfect."

*

They honked once as they drove off and before Alex had even had the chance to look for his door keys, Will wrenched it open and stood there, staring at him. Alex stared back.

Will stepped outside and closed the door behind him "Ben was in my battalion," he blurted out.

"Okay," replied Alex, not quite sure where this was leading. "Didn't you already know that? I mean, you spent a week together in the hospital."

"Yes, no, I mean, I don't know, I never asked, or if I did, I've forgotten what he said." Will was now pacing up and down the narrow platform just in front of their door.

"And that's a bad thing, or...?" asked Alex tentatively. He set down his bag, the strap of it already digging into his shoulder. He had a feeling this was going to take a little bit longer.

"No, not really. It doesn't really matter, I think," said Will, sounding very unsure of himself. "I don't like him dating Ruth," he suddenly added, taking Alex by surprise.

"What? Why?" he asked surprised, and then realised why they were having this conversation on their own door step instead of in their kitchen or living room. "Hang on, are they in there?"

Will looked guilty, but now he was standing directly in front of the door, effectively blocking Alex's way.

"What's going on?" Alex folded his arms, looking sternly at Will, who in his opinion was behaving slightly ridiculous the way he was hiding away from Ruth and Ben. Alex could only imagine how he must have jumped up off the couch the moment the head lights of Matt's car shone through the kitchen windows and the honk had sounded.

"He's in my battalion and they came to ask me whether I would march in the homecoming parades. And why does he know and I don't. Not to sound like an asshole, but I have a higher rank. Why is he informed but not me?"

Alex sighed. He hadn't expected this; he'd hoped he could open up the topic about the homecoming parades over a really nice and long breakfast Saturday morning.

"Because Ben doesn't have any family left. They called Eleanor this morning."

"How do you know?" asked Will.

"She called me at school." Alex knew this wasn't going to go down well and the dark look on Will's face confirmed it.

"She called you at school, while you were working? I'm home all day, with virtually nothing to do and she calls you." Will's voice grew louder and Alex didn't like having this kind of conversation out in the open where everybody could listen in to their problems. Neither did Will usually, but he supposed when having to choose between Ruth and Ben and some strangers, Will felt more inclined towards the strangers rather than have Ruth and Ben listen to their fight.

"Perhaps she feels you don't want to talk to her, seeing as you haven't called her once since you got back," hissed Alex at him. Will opened his mouth, but there was no retort.

"Will, what are you actually angry about? The parades? Ben being from your battalion? Your mum calling me?

What?" In the reflection of the window, Alex could see one of their neighbours peering out behind curtains, watching the scene unfolding on the other side of the street and right now, Alex just wanted to get inside the house.

Will didn't say anything, his eyes were darting left to right, as if he was trying to avoid Alex's eye.

"Do you even know?"

"It's Ben," said Will, still not looking at Alex.

"Can you tell me why?" asked Alex tentatively, but the moment the question was out of his mouth, Will had turned around and turned the door knob, to no avail.

"Give me your key," he said quietly, holding out his hand towards Alex, though his upper body was turned towards the door.

Alex sighed, and even though he would have liked to know what this had been all about, he also wanted to get inside, so he dug around for the key in his too large bag and handed it to Will. The door sprang open and before Alex had even stepped inside he could see Ruth anxiously waiting by the door to the living room. She was half hiding Ben from view who sat on the couch looking anxious.

"Hello, dearest brother. Did the parents leave you in one piece?" said Ruth. Her arms were folded, her long fingers resting on the upper arms comfortably and her long hair was falling loosely over her shoulders. She would look stunningly beautiful were it not for the scowling expression on her face she was directing at Will. Alex knew, and he supposed Will did as well, that in any other situation, Ruth would have steam-rolled over someone who pulled a stunt like Will just did, who disappeared into the kitchen without a word.

"Did you hear?" mouthed Alex at her.

Ruth nodded. Alex stepped closer, leaned in and hugged her. "Sorry, I don't know what's wrong."

"He suddenly doesn't like Ben, that's what's wrong," replied Ruth. "I thought they got along in the hospital."

Alex pulled back, just as Will was walking past them and out into the back garden, a cup of tea in his hands. "So did I," said Alex as the back door slid closed and Will sat down in his chair.

Ben got up from the couch and stood next to Ruth. He looked less pale now and generally had the aura of a happier person, despite the lines of worry on his face at this moment.

"I suppose this is our cue to leave," sighed Ruth. "Give him a smack on the head for me, will you?"

Alex nodded and let her pass. Ben held out her jacket for her and it seemed like they'd been doing that for years. As he opened the door to let them out Ruth kissed him on the cheek, and Ben grasped his hand to shake it. Before letting go, however, he leaned closer.

"This is about more than just the accident. So are his nightmares. There's something else," he said in a low voice.

"Yeah, I'm starting to think that too."

As the door closed, a dread fell on Alex. He let Will be, though he waited for him to join him in bed; saying good night and kissing him on the cheek, which he allowed.

It was another horrible night. At 4:30, Alex gave up on sleeping, simply laying there with a hand on Will's chest, rubbing it, sometimes touching his face or shoulder to avert the next nightmare. Alex sighed with relief every time Will's breathing calmed and his hands stopped gripping the sheets. It never lasted long though, the nightmares coming back in shorter intervals and by 6 o'clock, they were both wide awake.

33

"Do you want to go to the parades?"

Will had expected a different question after describing the events of three days ago, but it seemed Dr. Khan wasn't particularly interested in his feelings about Ben or the argument he'd had with Alex.

"I, um,..." He trailed off. He'd been so busy thinking about Ben and Alex that it hadn't really sunk in what going to the parades would mean.

"Simple question. One, it appears, you haven't answered for yourself yet, let alone told Alex the answer."

Will felt like a schoolboy being reprimanded for not knowing what 2+2 equals. He wasn't sure.

"Let me give you your options, Mr Collins. First option: You stay at home, knowing full well that these parades are happening on that day and you won't be able to stop thinking about it, that I can guarantee. It will most likely make you feel miserable and won't in any way aid you.

Second option: You go to the parade as a spectator, which will also make you feel miserable because you will feel excluded from everything. You'll see your comrades marching by and will feel like you're not a part of them anymore-"

"Technically I'm-"

"I haven't finished," silenced Dr. Khan him.

Third option: You'll march alongside your platoon, alongside your comrades. You will once more feel like you're a part of them. You will notice that your injury doesn't change the fact that you and these men are comrades for life. You fought a war together after all. You will be proud and – and this is the most important thing – there will be a sort of closure. You'll be marching as a returnee, as someone who has come home. After that, in every parade you will be a veteran, which isn't less worthy, but it's still not quite the same." Dr. Khan looked at him over the edge of his spectacles. It seemed condescending, as if he wanted to say: Why are we even talking about this, of course, you're going to that parade.

"What if that closure isn't happening?" asked Will.

Dr Khan leaned forward. "Then we'll deal with that when the time comes, but if you don't go, you're denying yourself the possibility of closure right from the beginning."

Butterflies filled up his stomach and goosebumps crawled up his skin at the thought of going to that parade, but he couldn't deny the logic behind the doctor's thinking.

"That's that," said the doctor, placing his pen on the desk, next to his file. This was the point where things were off the record, as Dr Khan had explained in the first session, and Will thought he knew what question would follow.

"Do you want to talk about it today?"

His answer was still the same, even more so now. "No."

"Have you told Alex?"

"No, of course not." said Will.

Dr Khan nodded. "Okay. Then tell me about your first year as a private."

34

Will felt completely drained when he left the doctor's office and headed home. The long walk along the river returned some of his energy, but also brought with it a headache as well as a feeling of panic. He stopped by the willow tree, watching the geese, hoping that they would give him answers, but they tended to be very quiet and it wasn't different that day.

The front of the house was dark, only the small light above the door shining in the dusk. The door wasn't locked and as soon as he entered he saw torches through the window, lightening up their garden. Alex was sitting in his garden chair. He looked up as he heard Will's footsteps.

"How was it?"

"Strange again, but not as strange as the first time anymore."

Alex nodded and didn't press the matter for which Will was grateful. Though Alex could be nosy if he wanted to, he also had the decency to accept when someone wasn't feeling like sharing.

"Garden torches?"

Alex smiled. "Too cheesy? They were on offer. I thought they looked nice."

The light of the torches doused the garden in orange, spreading a warm feeling throughout. It looked beautiful already and Will couldn't wait till the flowers and bushes were in bloom. "They do. You actually did good."

Alex raised his eyebrows. "Is that a compliment, from you, directed at me, about the garden?"

"Well, not the garden, it's more the torches," said Will, smiling at Alex's happy surprise.

"Yeah, yeah. Whatever you say. I did good. I could have bought a garden gnome instead."

Will made a noise of disgust that made Alex laugh. "Don't you dare."

Alex crossed his fingers to calm Will. He wouldn't even think about wasting his money on a garden gnome, knowing full well Will would just dump them in the bin first chance he got.

"Alex?"

"Yes?" Alex's smile disappeared as he saw the look on Will's face.

"I'm going to take part in the parades."

Alex sighed and nodded. "You would have had to anyway." He leaned down to pick up a letter off the ground. "Andrew would have had a say in it, otherwise. He sounds very insistent in this letter that you should be there by his side. He's looking forward to it."

Will took the letter and pulled the two small sheets out of the envelope. "You read it?"

"It was addressed to both of us," said Alex. "You read, I'll make you a cup of tea and get started on dinner."

Will nodded absent-mindedly. A pang of guilt at not having written Andrew engulfed him for a second, but it was almost immediately overcome by a rush of affection as he started reading:

Will,

This place hasn't quite been the same without you. Less fun. The rest of the platoon isn't quite so ready to make cynical comments about commanders or to share jokes in the Humvee while under attack as you had always been. They didn't even laugh at my whale joke. A travesty, I know.

This lack of fun did give me time to think, and I've decided that this is it for me. No more. I know we've said we wanted to rise above and beyond, but things changed and you know as well as I do what I'm talking about. So this will be it and afterwards, I'm just going to have to see what I'll do.

We're coming home soon, though it feels far away still. So I'll be seeing you soon and we'll be walking in the parade together, whether you like it or not, I've saved a spot for you.

See you April 11th. I won't be able to leave barracks before then. Don't even think about visiting. I don't want you near this place, we'll see enough of each other for the rest of our lives once I'm out of here.

Your second best friend (one day I'll be having a fight with that Cohen), Andy

P.S. Alex, have you done it yet?

Will looked up in confusion. Alex was standing right next to him, Will not having heard him approach. He held out a steaming cup of tea that Will accepted dazedly.

"Have you done what?" he asked.

"Nothing," replied Alex, walking away.

"Alex! Have you done what?"

Alex turned around in exasperation. "You're not supposed to know yet and Andrew wasn't supposed to blab."

Will waved the letter, spilling hot tea and splashing the ground with it. "This isn't exactly blabbing. I don't know anything, that's teasing, that's torturing – not telling me anything."

"Well, then you know how I feel," said Alex before he could stop himself. This time, Will didn't stop him from entering the house again and he didn't follow.

35

If Alex expected Will to comment on his exclamation he was wrong to do so. Instead, Will pulled back again, not as thoroughly as before but it was still far away enough from that night when they'd almost had sex, and frustration found a deep anchor again.

Will went to Dr Khan every other day, and Alex wasn't sure what he was hoping for, or what Will was hoping for, but to him, it still somehow felt as if nothing was coming of it. He tried telling himself that it hadn't been that long, that it was only the fourth or fifth or sixth meeting. But every time Will came home from these meetings, he barely talked, retreating with a book or going straight to bed. Alex felt like they had taken a hundred steps backwards within only a matter of days.

Instructions for the parade in Shrewsbury and Market Drayton arrived – Market Drayton was to be first, though Will had said that the Shrewsbury parade would be enough for him – and local radio stations as well as some national TV channels began talking about the return of Operation Herrick 13 soldiers.

It was after the fifth time of hearing 'these brave soldiers deserve all our support' on the radio that Alex had enough of their silent trot and Will's hardened facial expressions.

"You want to go see Andrew tomorrow?" he asked over dinner, after they'd spent the Sunday in separate places all over the house – Alex preparing lessons and Will working in the garden, or Alex cooking lunch and Will reading upstairs.

Will shook his head. "No, he said he'd like to acclimate himself to his surroundings before seeing me. I think he's being nostalgic."

"Nostalgic?" asked Alex, confused about the use of that word in the given context.

"It was always 'when we get home, we'll do this and that'. We always thought along the lines of 'we – home - party', but not 'boom – I injured – home' and 'boredom – sadness – orders – home' and then meet somewhere in the middle of Tern Hill or something. He said he'd like to at least have the party feeling we've been talking about, so I'll see him Tuesday."

It made sense in their strange kind of way. It was those moments that Alex could understand people who'd told him to be careful when dating a soldier as they could be peculiar people.

"What will you do tomorrow?"

"Go to Dr Khan. I've got an appointment at 9. And then Ruth asked me for lunch, so I'll meet her in town at 12, which I'm sure is your doing," said Will.

"No, it wasn't. I had no idea. Did she say what she wants?"

Will looked surprised. "No clue."

"Be careful what you tell her," said Alex with a mischievous smile that made Will laugh.

"Don't worry, our dark secrets are safe with me."

By the time they'd done the dishes and made another cup of tea, it seemed as if nothing had happened, as was wont with them. They fought loudly, they fought in silence and then they talked and everything was back to normal – more or less.

That night, Will even curled up on the couch with Alex again, letting him read out loud.

36

Alex couldn't help check his watch more frequently than usual and his stomach overturned itself when both hands of the watch moved to 12. He regretted not having called Ruth the night before to ask what she was planning on doing, but being able to lie on the couch with Will and read to him took priority.

His students were reading Cold War sources and analysing them, which meant he could let his thoughts wander to all the possible things Ruth might be wanting from Will. The most plausible thing was to ask him to be nice to Ben.

Time went by too slowly, the break seemed longer than usual and on other days, he would have appreciated it, but today, he just wanted to get home and find out what Ruth wanted.

By the end of seventh period, Abby was laughing at him. "Alex, you look like a rabbit being hunted. Calm down, it's your sister and your boyfriend talking. What can happen?"

"It's my sister, Abby. A lot can happen," said Alex. He rubbed his eyes. "The last and only time they met without me was when she told him what kind of a man my father is. He didn't speak to me for a week because he'd felt I lied to him about my parentage, about the kind of money my dad has and that I'm not quite as white middle class as he had expected. Right now, we can't afford that kind of silence. We're off and on speaking terms as it is."

"Are you?" asked Abby, looking shocked.

"I keep saying stupid things and then it's all distance again and not talking much. I mean it's better, generally, but it's not good yet." Alex paused, thinking back to Ben's statement, thinking back to the evening after Will's first session with Dr Khan. "There's something else, something he's not telling me."

"Then, wouldn't it be a good thing if maybe he tells Ruth?"

"He's supposed to tell me," said Alex.

Abby patted his arm. "Next to his parents, you're the most important person in his life. That makes it so much harder."

Alex sighed. "I know. You're not the first one to say that."

"Who else said it?" asked Abby, as they left the teachers' lounge and climbed down the stairs.

"Ben."

Here and there, they waved goodbye to colleagues or nodded at students who'd never do such things as wave at a teacher, but also didn't want to seem like they had no respect – at least as long as they were alone, finding themselves passing two teachers.

"I like him," said Abby. "There's a sincerity about him, and I don't know, maturity? It's rather touching." They reached her car, a disgrace to the colour yellow, but the booth was roomy, which is all that mattered to someone who carried around a lot of things. There were cardboards in the booth, plus boxes full of pens and different coloured paper.

"When did you meet him?"

"Friday. Ruth invited us for dinner. She felt Will wouldn't appreciate it, which is probably why she's meeting him today," said Abby, looking at Alex meaningfully.

"Yeah, yeah. Take me home and I'll find out."

37

Ruth's car was parked in front of their house. Normally, Abby would have come in too, but she'd promised Matt that they would meet at four o'clock to look for a new couch and it was already 10 past.

Alex unlocked the door, looking forward to his couch where he could sprawl and just do nothing for the rest of the day.

"ALEX!" The yell came from the kitchen and seconds later, Ruth was standing right in front of him, eyes blazing.

"What?" He looked at her in shock. Her cheeks were blushed and her shoulders pulled back, her high heels did the rest to make her seem a lot taller than himself.

"You were planning on asking him to marry you and he knows and this Andrew guy knows and how the fuck do I not know anything? I'm your sister."

His bag dropped from his shoulder in shock and he gasped for breath for a good twenty seconds before regaining the ability to speak. "How do you know? How do YOU know?" he asked Will.

Will squirmed and looked towards the ground. "Well, there was Andrew's letter and I had a vague idea and we talked on the phone and I asked him and he folded and told me and I also kind of found the ring."

"You – wha- ugh," stuttered Alex, throwing up his arms. "And then you tell her?"

"You should have told me. Again, I'm your sister. I'm the bloody bridesmaid," said Ruth, almost making Alex laugh with her indignation.

"Abby's going to be the bridesmaid," he said, just to tease her some more. Furiously, she stepped closer.

"Oh no, she's not. I am. She can be flower girl."

"First, I'd have to say 'yes'," interrupted Will.

Ruth flipped around so fast she hit Alex in the face with her hair. "Is that even questionable?"

A tension unlike the one before built up between them and Will's eyes darted between Alex and Ruth.

"Would you? Say yes?" asked Alex quietly, pulling Will's gaze towards him.

A pause, and then-

"Probably."

Ruth turned around fully now, essentially blocking Alex's way. "Probably? Probably? There's no probably. Yes or no?" Her voice was very commanding, as if she thought she'd achieve her ends better that way. But whatever orders Will had followed in his military life, it didn't mean he'd blindly follow any order.

"Well, not like this; in the hallway with you standing between us," he said, sounding just as indignant as Ruth had mere seconds before. She faced Alex again, jabbing a finger at his chest.

"Right, do it, properly, and soon. And you better say 'yes'," she added with a glare at Will. "I can't believe you didn't tell me, Alex. I'm angry, and not talking to you. See you tomorrow at the parade." She still kissed him on the cheek and waved at Will, before angrily swiping her hair back – hitting Alex in the face again – and leaving the house.

Awkward silence followed, Will fumbling with his T-shirt while Alex was too stunned to move.

"You weren't supposed to know," said Alex, not sure what else to say.

Will stepped forward, right in front of Alex, so that he was looking at him and his breath tickled Alex's skin.

"You were going to ask me when I got back, right? When I would have gotten back, yesterday."

Alex nodded. "The original plan was to ask you tomorrow at the Shrewsbury parade. Andrew knew that because he was supposed to help. My guess is he assumed I'd already done it."

"Yeah, he said that."

Alex couldn't decide between feeling guilty about the entire situation, especially that he hadn't asked him yet; and feeling aroused at the closeness of their bodies. Will often used the height advantage to tease Alex this way, standing close in front of him with his breath tickling Alex's skin.

"Don't do it tomorrow," said Will quietly. "Please."

"I won't."

Will leaned in and softly placed his lips on Alex's. It was chaste and quick and before Alex knew it, Will was walking away from him.

"I like the ring by the way. Good choice."

Alex smiled and felt like the idiot fool in love that he'd been years ago.

38

They were tangled up in each other when the alarm clock rang. Alex's top half of his head was wedged against Will's chest, the other half pressed into the bed. His left arm was squeezed in between their bodies, while his right lay loosely over Will's hips. He himself was curled up in a tight embrace, Will's legs gripping his left one. It was hot and skin was glued to skin, but as soon as he opened his eyes he wanted to close them again to relish the position they were in. He took a deep breath, capturing Will's musky scent mixed with watermelon from his shampoo.

Will stirred; the alarm clock ringing shrilly wasn't going to give up unless one of them moved. Will pulled away, dragging Alex with him half-way. His hand found the alarm clock and the ringing stopped to be replaced by a deep sleepy groan. Alex's head was pleasantly placed on Will's arm. Except suddenly it wasn't, Will having pulled it out from under him rather violently. Alex just about saw how Will ran into the bathroom and banged the door shut before he heard a retching sound. He was out of bed immediately.

"Will? Are you okay?" He opened the door and found Will hanging over the toilet, just reaching up to flush it. "What's wrong?"

Will coughed before replying. "Nothing, I'm fine."

Alex grabbed a towel of the rack and handed it to Will. "Are you sure you want to do this today?"

Will wiped his mouth. There were tears in his eyes from the force of the vomiting and he sniffed. "No," he mumbled into the towel so that Alex could barely understand it. "But I'm going to do it anyway."

He stood up, threw the towel in the laundry basket and went back into the bedroom. "You take a shower first, you have to get to work," he said, with his back towards Alex.

Alex succumbed to the urge and took two steps closer. He gently pushed Will's arms away so that his own could wrap around. He aligned their bodies, chest pressed to back, and kissed the skin at the base of the neck.

"You'll be fine," he whispered. Will took a deep breath and Alex could feel the nervous heart beating under his hands. "You'll be fine." He extricated himself, his hand moving over Will's chest and lingering on his hipbone reassuringly.

Alex showered quickly, but by the time he was dressed and went downstairs, Will was gone. A small piece of paper lay on the kitchen counter:

Had to go for a walk. I'll see you later. —Will

Alex crumbled up the piece of paper and threw it away. He'd known this was a bad idea.

39

Some of his students were wearing yellow ribbons on their bags or jackets, or had them wrapped around the arm like you would a black band for a funeral. He couldn't remember this happening for any other homecoming parade; it comforted him.

Abby seemed on tenterhooks around him all morning and he wasn't sure how much of his inner tension he was exuding. First period annoyed him and he let it out on one of his students, though apologised profusely afterwards. Second period was just purely tantalising and if his students were concerned about his behaviour, they didn't show it. He knew it was highly unprofessional, but he always said teachers are humans too, and he was just all too human that day.

Abby walked into his classroom as soon as the bell rang, which meant she had ended her class early.

"Let's go."

40

As the parade was going right past their school grounds, the headmaster had arranged for all students and teachers to line the street around it and cheer the soldiers on. They had also never done that before, but Operation Herrick 13 had been special for a lot of people in this school – students and teachers alike. Two of the dead soldiers had been the fathers of students of this school, and there were several more wounded connected to it. It had been a tough year for everyone. It was easy to forget sometimes when overwhelmed with your own personal problems, but the way the students lined up in orderly fashion and took out their flags and small banners brought everything into perspective.

In the distance, they could already hear the marching song of the regiment. Abby took his hand in hers and squeezed it tightly.

"Homecoming," she whispered. "He came home."

Alex looked at her, frowning slightly. "I know."

"Now it's final."

Alex nodded. Now it was final; he couldn't help but feel relief.

Some of the kids began to cheer and as he looked, Alex saw the band coming into view as they turned the corner. Will was second company, third platoon. Ben was first company, second platoon. Ruth had said she wanted to wait by the Abbey where the parade would end, followed by a mass inside. She'd take them home after.

The band walked past, the sound of the bagpipes and drums ringing in his ears. The children cheered and waved their flags. The first company came by, the beat of their feet on the ground hypnotising.

He almost missed Ben, who was marching in the outer left row, uniform ill-fitting as if he'd lost ten kilos since he'd last worn it. Alex wondered whether Will would look the same. The pace of the march was fast, a clockwork not quite in sync with the time, counting ahead of the minutes.

Before he knew it, Abby was squeezing his hand again and he looked up to see Will in the outer right row. Andrew was right beside him, a mountain amongst hills. From where the crowd was standing, Will's injured eye was barely discernible. You would miss it if you didn't look for it.

Just as he passed, one of the Yr7 boys standing to Alex's right, raised his voice and whooped.

"Welcome home! You are heroes."

Abby's hand jerked and Alex looked at her, Will moving on and walking out of sight.

"What?"

Abby frowned, looking at the boy who was still cheering and shouting. "I could have sworn Will lost his footing for a second when Geoffrey yelled. Like he was stunned by it. You didn't see it?"

Alex shook his head, whilst trying to catch another glimpse of Will. "I was looking at Geoffrey."

The last of the parade was passing them now, closely followed by some supporting family and friends walking towards the Abbey with them. The children's applause died down and a high murmur started up. The headmaster gave the sign and Alex, Abby and the other teachers were ushering the students back inside. The old janitor Williamson was making pretend sweeping motions directed at the children, dusting them together and into the school building. Some students laughed and giggled, others ran ahead in order to not be last inside.

If periods one and two had been bad, three, four, five and six were pure horror. Alex knew he should have taken the day off, should have played sick and waited by the Abbey for Will.

Should have, should have, should have...

41

"Do you want me to come with you?" asked Abby, though she didn't look like she was expecting a 'yes', sitting back in the driver's seat, hands folded in her lap.

"No, I expect he'll want to be alone. I wonder how he feels." Alex ruffled his hair, messing it up badly. Abby reached over and flattened it again.

"You're going to find out in a second. Perhaps, this was a good idea, maybe it did help him," she said. "You've got to stop worrying before it's due."

"I'm not worrying. I'm weighing the possible outcomes of certain situations against another and then prepare myself to what I expect to happen."

"Still not healthy for your mind," said Abby. She opened the seat belt for him, effectively kicking him out of the car. "Call me."

"Will do," said Alex, grabbing his bag from the backseat and getting out of the car.

The front door slammed shut behind him due to the draft coming in from the open sliding door leading out into the garden. Will was sitting in his chair, still in his uniform, seemingly enjoying the April sun. In Alex's chair sat Andrew and judging by the way he was leaning towards Will and gesturing wildly he was either telling a huge story or trying to appeal to Will in some way.

The sand crunched under his feet and Andrew turned his head to look at him. He smiled, but it was only a half-smile. "Alex, nice to see you again."

"I could say the same, well, if you hadn't spoiled –"

"Yes, yes, I know," said Andrew. "I should have just kept my mouth shut. Sorry about that." He stood up and Alex noticed that he wasn't in his uniform trousers. Following Alex's eyes, Andrew smoothed the sweat pants he was wearing.

"My trousers are in the wash. Something happened." He looked at Will as he said it. Andrew stepped closer, leaning down so that his mouth was close to Alex's ear. "He didn't have much of a breakfast, did he?"

Alex jerked his head around, watching Will, who sat there unmoving, staring ahead at the daffodils.

"I'll be in the kitchen. I'm hungry."

He thumped Alex on the shoulder hard, making him stumble forwards slightly. He used the movement to walk to his chair and sit down.

Will still didn't look at him. His eyes were red and there were visible tear stains running down his cheek. His Corporal insignia had been torn off, the threads hanging limply like unwanted entrails.

"Will? What happened?"

His eyes were roaming the ground like those of a wild panicking animal and his breathing was shallow and fast.

"It didn't help, did it?" asked Alex, already knowing the answer.

Will shook his head, but still his eyes didn't meet Alex's.

"What is it?" Alex grabbed the chair and pulled it around so that he was almost facing Will as he sat down. Will stared at the roses in the far corner, unrelenting even when Alex touched his arm.

Will, you're going to have to tell me one day," insisted Alex.

"I'm not allowed to tell you, you know that."

Alex leaned back in his chair, sighing. "I know. But I also know that this is killing you. Have you told Dr. Khan?"

"I'm not allowed to tell him either."

"Does Andy know?"

"Yes."

Alex ruffled his hair, his hands needing to do something. He felt utterly helpless, even though, somehow, it all made sense too. The distancing, the nightmares, the lack of conversation. "So is this how it's going to be? And I just have to deal with your bad moments, never to question, 'cause I'm not allowed to know? You're just going to let me sit next to you, say nothing, do nothing, ever wondering what the fuck is going on?"

"He said we were his heroes," interrupted Will, his voice cracking at the last word.

It was abrupt and stopped Alex in his tracks. "I know, I heard," he said in a soft voice.

"I didn't sign up for that." Will leaned forward, hiding his eyes behind his hands. "I didn't sign up for that," he repeated, shaking his head.

Alex leaned over and touched his shoulder, but Will pulled away immediately.

"Don't."

Alex reached for him again, more insistent this time. "Will-"

"No, don't. Please." Will jumped up and walked three paces away from him. "Fuck." It was a whisper only, but Alex heard it. It was worse than Will pulling away from him.

Will stared at the rose bushes he had planted, as if they could give him answers. But they were still barren, empty, barely any life in them and certainly no answers. Will suddenly shook his head violently and erupted. "What I did in Afghanistan, that was not my job. My job stopped being my job the moment I set foot in Afghanistan. I signed up to protect my country, my family, my friends, to get rid of the bad guys and make sure that our world is perhaps a little bit safer and the things I thought I had to do for that – those were the things I could have cleared with my conscience. Kill the terrorists, actually kill the bad guys, if necessary. I could have done that. I was ready to do that. But it wasn't like that, it just wasn't. They used us and they turned us into something we were not supposed to be. That's why he's quitting." Will gestured towards the house where Andrew was making something to eat, possibly fighting with his own peace of mind.

Alex got up from his seat and took a step towards him and when Will didn't say anything he took another and another, until he was standing right in front of him. He raised Will's head with both his hands to make him look him in the eye.

"Today was a mistake," said Will and began opening his jacket buttons. "I shouldn't have worn this, I shouldn't have walked in the parade. It was stupid, I didn't deserve it, I didn't belong. I'm not a hero, I've never felt less like a hero." He threw the jacket to the ground. His shoulders sagged and he suddenly looked very small in his black T-shirt and the too large army trousers. "But that's how everyone sees us, don't they? That or it's the other side. That we're murderers, killers who have disrupted a country and caused unnecessary harm. And you know what, yes, we did. Yes, I did. I'm sure I did. In two cases I'm a hundred percent sure, in one case, I'm eighty percent sure." He paused. "I caused unnecessary harm. And that was my fault."

"You were acting on orders, weren't you?"

"Not really, not specifically."

Alex frowned.

"You know how it is. We get general orders that carry throughout the entire mission and then you make judgement calls. Those calls are mine, and mine alone. And I made the wrong ones." He looked up at the sky, sighing heavily. "And now they're in my dreams." His voice sounded heavy, raspier and yet, almost timid. He was telling a secret that weighed on him.

And if anyone had asked him later how he knew, Alex wouldn't have been able to explain it. But his brain suddenly made the connection. Little 12-year-old George waving a flag in the parade flashed before his eyes and Abby's concerned face when she commented on Will's reaction went through his head and somehow, he knew.

He didn't know what to say. If someone came into school and shot one of his students, he would be repulsed, angry, distraught. But this was Will and Alex couldn't help thinking that whatever had happened, it had helped get Will home in the end.

"You shot a kid." It came out before Alex could stop himself. He needed to know. Will's eyes widened in surprise, confirming Alex's suspicion. Will had shot a child. Probably no older than innocent, funny George in Year 7.

Will nodded and Alex started pacing around the garden. Will had shot a child, perhaps more than one, but Alex wasn't sure he wanted to know.

"I shot a kid," said Will, the words carrying across the garden at no more than a whisper; and the rawness of those four words hit Alex right in the chest. He had to take a deep breath. He crouched down, running his hands through his hair.

"I shot him in the head. I thought he was armed, but maybe he wasn't. I think they'd made it look like he was so that I would shoot him. Some of them, some of the people we fought, they just wanted proof, I think. Proof that we were shooting innocent children now, that we hadn't come to bring peace. Whatever that means. It doesn't mean anything to me. Not anymore, because I shot a kid and I see him at night, he's in every nightmare. It doesn't always look like him, but it's always him. It's always him. I'm not hero. I'm..." Will lost his voice in a cough and Alex got up and turned to face him. He was clenching his chest, brushing away tears forcefully.

Something tickled Alex's cheek and he realised that he was crying too, though he wasn't sure what he was crying about. The child that he didn't know? Will?

He walked over to Will and held his face in his hands. He didn't know what he was looking for. Will's good eye was avoiding his gaze and he had his arms crossed, as if to shut everything out. Or to shut himself in.

"It wasn't your fault," Alex finally said and immediately knew it was the wrong thing to say. Will's shoulders tensed.

"I pulled the trigger."

Alex shook his head slowly. He felt like he'd never known how to think, as if, what used to come so easy, was simply gone. "But how much of a choice did you really have? Did you really have a choice, or was the choice for you and Andy and Jack to die? And perhaps more people? Would it have been you instead of the kid?"

"I don't know," Will answered. "In that situation, I couldn't have known for sure without endangering everyone else."

"So you made a judgement call."

"Yes."

There was a pause and Alex could hear the swans flying across the river, their powerful wings straining the air and making it ring out.

"I'm glad you did," whispered Alex.

Will's arm twitched as he wanted to raise it and place it around Alex, to hug him, but he thought better of it in the last second. Alex shook his head, unable to think of what else to do.

Alex tightened his grip on Will's head, his fingers leaving dents in the skin. "I'm sorry, I shouldn't have said that. But ... don't you think you've been punished enough? Because I think you have."

Will stared into Alex's eyes, unblinking, as if he wanted to find out something.

"I just want you to come back to me. Please come back to me." Will raised his eyebrows ever so slightly before a frown formed on his brow. "Properly."

They looked at each other and Alex tried to not blink, somehow thinking that would reassure Will, that it would make him feel better. He didn't know why.

"I shot a kid." said Will.

Alex swallowed before answering. "I know."

"And you're okay with that?"

"I don't know yet." Alex lowered his head. He tried to think, but still nothing came. He did not know. "The one thing I do know is that I want you here with me."

Will's arms found their way around Alex's shoulders and pulled him in tight. It was taking Alex's breath away.

"Okay." It was quieter than anything else Will had said so far.

42

It was the middle of the night, moonlight shining in through the open window. At some point during the afternoon, Andrew had ushered them back inside and fed them with fettuccini and pesto. Will, exhausted, went to bed while Andrew filled Alex in on the events of the afternoon and waited for the dryer to finish with his trousers.

Alex didn't do anything for work, deciding to call in sick in the morning. He needed a day, perhaps two and he thought, so did Will. They could go to Snowdonia for the weekend, climb the mountains.

Will was fast asleep, curled on his side, when he entered the bedroom. Quietly, he undressed and climbed into bed, but he didn't shut his eyes and instead, watched Will sleep. He listened to his breathing, slightly irregular at times with a quiet wheezing still wedging its way outside. Every now and then he furrowed his brow and Alex tensed, waiting for Will to wake up in shock or even screaming, but he didn't.

At two a.m. − Alex was after all slowly drifting off − Will awoke. He coughed once, jerking Alex out of drowsiness.

"Sorry," whispered Will. "Didn't want to wake you."

Alex smiled. "I wasn't really sleeping yet."

"Were you watching me?"

Alex was glad it was too dark to see properly, even with the moon lighting up the room. "How are you feeling?"

Will squirmed slightly, but stopped when Alex laid a hand on his. "Better, I think."

"You think?"

"Better," said Will more firmly this time. "How are you?"

"Still not quite sure. It's a lot to take in if I'm honest."

"You never saw it that way, did you?" asked Will.

"Yeah, no. It's like I was shutting that part out completely, without even realising. And I shouldn't have. I'm a History Teacher for crying out loud, if there's one thing I know it's what any war involves."

"14."

It took Alex a moment to realise what that number meant. At the same time, he wasn't sure that it meant that much to him, though it probably did to Will. To him, it was 14 different faces.

"Do you see them all in your dreams?"

"No. It's just the kid."

Will closed his eyes and Alex wondered what he saw. "He doesn't seem to go away."

"Are you going to see Dr Khan tomorrow?" asked Alex.

"Yeah, I think I should."

"Can I come with you?"

Will was silent for a long time, before he quietly whispered: "Yes."

He scooted closer, so that their foreheads were touching. They didn't speak for the longest time, but neither closed their eyes nor moved; until Will yawned and detached his forehead from Alex's. Alex laughed quietly.

"You're cute."

"No I'm not."

"Yes, you are, sometimes. In a dorky kind of way."

Will snorted. "You're totally ruining the compliment."

Alex laughed again.

"Go to sleep, Alex. You have work in the morning."

Alex shook his head, which looked and felt strange lying on his side with half his face hidden by the pillow. "I'm going to be sick in the morning."

"Are you?" asked Will with a smirk.

"Yeah, I'm not feeling too good, my throat hurts and my nose is itchy," said Alex, coughing and sniffing once for proof. Will patted his chest in fake sympathy.

"I see you're concerned," said Alex, pretending to be hurt by Will's lack of genuine care.

"Always, my dearest Alex." They both laughed, making the bed shake.

The thought came suddenly and he only spared a second thinking about Ruth yelling at him about how he should have done it properly – he felt like there'd be no better moment, no grander gesture that would be more perfect than this.

"Will?" he asked.

"Alex?" Will was smiling at him, still coming down from laughing.

"Will you marry me?"

Will sobered up immediately, his face hardened, and Alex wasn't sure he liked how quickly it had happened.

"Didn't we agree you wouldn't ask today?" whispered Will, suddenly looking so very small and lost again.

"It's not that today anymore," replied Alex, nervously waiting for the actual reply. He didn't want to hear probably again. Slowly but surely, Will's expression turned softer and smoother, the worry lines disappeared and were replaced by other lines.

"You're an idiot."

Alex's face lit up with a smile. "I'll take that as a 'yes'."

Will shook his head in astonishment, but his smile now covered his entire face, from lips to eyes. "You're still an idiot."

They kissed again, longer than before, deeper than before, until Will yawned again. "Go to sleep," said Alex.

"What about my ring?" demanded Will indignantly.

"Really?"

"You just asked me. It's custom for there to be a ring involved."

"You just called me an idiot instead of simply saying 'yes'. Not sure you deserve the ring."

Will rolled his eyes. "Okay, let's do this again over breakfast, properly."

"Okay," said Alex. "But it's still a 'yes', right?"

"Jesus, you're a pest. YES!"